Dead Giveaways

Andrew Donkin

Illustrations by Paul Fisher-Johnson

Dead Giveaways

How real life crimes are solved by amazing
scientific evidence, personality profiling and
paranormal investigations

Andrew Donkin

Illustrations by Paul Fisher-Johnson

ELEMENT
CHILDREN'S BOOKS

SHAFTESBURY, DORSET · BOSTON, MASSACHUSETTS · MELBOURNE, VICTORIA

ACKNOWLEDGMENTS

My thanks to all those people who generously gave their time and resources to help with the writing of this book.

Particularly: Helen Chevallier, Alex Hall, Stephen O'Brien and the staff of his Frederick Lab, and Chris Robinson.

Special thanks to paranormal investigator Lorne Mason for his help with the sections of text dealing with psychic cases.

A grateful nod of the head to: Jamie Finch, Ron Fogelman, Sophie Hicks, Lee Sullivan, Lottie Rauch, and Special Agent Angharad Claire Randall.

Thanks as always to Paul Fisher-Johnson for his excellent illustrations.

And, most importantly, another huge thank you and much love to Suzy Jenvey and Scooby-Doo.

First published in the UK by Element Children's Books in 1998
Shaftesbury, Dorset SP7 8BP

Published in the USA in 1998 by Element Books Inc.
PO Box Box 830, Boston MA

Published in Australia in 1998 by Element Books Ltd for
Penguin Books Australia Ltd, 487 Maroodah Highway,
Ringwood, Victoria 3134

British Library Cataloguing in Publication data available.
Library of Congress Cataloging in Publication data available.

ISBN 1 901881 059

Text design by Dorchester Typesetting Group Ltd
Printed and bound in Great Britain by
Biddles Ltd, Guildford and King's Lynn

Contents

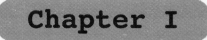

Chapter I

Introduction

*Y*ou are a detective. It is after midnight and your phone is ringing. A voice tells you that there has been an incident and that you are the nearest senior officer to the scene of the crime.

You get dressed and walk out into the night. It is raining and it takes three attempts to get your car started because of the cold. You drive for six minutes as the rain gets worse.

When you get to the scene, two police cars and a van are already parked outside. Their revolving flashing lights pierce the dark. It is a large house in a nice part of town. You show your police ID and walk past the uniformed officers guarding the front door.

Inside, the house is swarming with people. More uniformed officers patrol the garden. Crime scene officers in special clothing are dusting a window frame for fingerprints.

You walk into the main room. On the floor is a dead body. You do not flinch. You do not even pause. You lean down and take a close look at the victim, being careful not to touch anything.

A pool of blood is slowly spreading across the floor from the victim's head wound.

A crime-scene officer examines a large glass paperweight that's probably the murder weapon. You watch as he uses a fine white powder to brush for fingerprints. Then he shakes his head. It has been wiped clean.

You stand up and take a slow look around the room. You try to imagine it without the police officers. You try to imagine the last moments of the victim's life.

It is your job to catch the killer. Where are you going to start?

You realize you are in the way of the police photographer and step outside into the hallway. One of the crime scene officers walks towards you holding a small plastic bag. It looks empty, but she tells you that she has found three strands of black hair in the hall. You look back at the victim. She is a blonde and she lived alone.

Another officer is taking a photograph of a shoe print found in the kitchen. It is large, almost certainly made by a man. Judging by how wet the print is, it was made within the last few hours.

These fragments of evidence are valuable pieces in a murder jigsaw, but only you can put them together to see the whole picture . . .

Dead Giveaways is about how police catch criminals and about how criminals catch themselves.

Every crime scene holds vital, hidden clues – both physical and psychological – pointing towards the person that did it.

Physical material – like tiny hairs or invisible fingerprints – can be used to link him or her to the scene of the crime.

The method of the crime and the choice of victim will reveal elements of the criminal's character and state of mind.

A crime that creates intense emotions, like kidnaping or murder, may also leave other traces. Information is recorded in the very fabric of the crime scene or on the murder weapon. Sometimes psychics or dowsers claim they are able to read such information and discover what happened.

Today, police forces around the world have more weapons available in their fight against crime than ever before. As crime-detection becomes ever more complex, detectives are learning to use every method of investigation at their disposal.

THE CRIME SCENE

Proper examination of the crime scene is probably the most important part of any investigation.

The first task is to secure the crime scene so that no evidence is taken out or brought into the area. The police photographer will get to work early in the proceedings to record as much detail as possible before the crime-scene officers take over. Most police forces today will also shoot footage of the scene on videotape using a hand-held camera.

A sketch or plan of the room will be made with particular attention paid to the location and the relative position of the victim.

If there is a body at the scene then the most important question that the investigating officers need to ask is: What was the cause of death?

A detailed examination of the body will take place later in the form of a post-mortem.

NAMING THE VICTIM

The first task in any murder investigation is always to establish the identity of the victim beyond any doubt. Usually this
is easily done, but occasionally a murderer will go to great
lengths to make the corpse unrecognizable in the hope of
throwing off the police.

In our first case – the Luton Sack Murder – an unidentified body was central to the investigation. The killer was only
brought to justice by a combination of good detective work,
skillful handling of evidence, and perseverance.

THE LUTON SACK MURDER

On the afternoon of November 19, 1943 a sack was
dragged from the shallows of the River Lea near Luton in
Bedfordshire, UK. Inside was the dead body of a woman.

She was about thirty-five years old and had been dead for less than twenty-four hours.

The woman had absolutely no identification. Her clothes, jewelry, and even her false teeth had all been removed.

Police appealed to the general public for information through newspapers reports. A total of nine people came forward claiming to know who she was, but all of them were proved to be mistaken in their identifications.

The body would have stayed nameless if not for the efforts of Detective Chief Inspector William Chapman. Where other officers might have given up or filed the case under "unsolved," Chapman would not let it rest. He ordered his men to search local garbage dumps looking for women's clothes discarded at around the time of the murder.

On one dump, they found a dirty black coat that had, rather suspiciously, been deliberately ripped to shreds. The remains of the coat had a tattered dry-cleaning tag attached to it, numbered V 2247.

THE MISSING WIFE

Thanks to the local branch of the dry cleaners Sketchley's, police soon traced the coat's owner as being Mrs. Caroline Manton who lived at 14 Regent Street, Luton.

When investigating officers called, Horace "Bertie" Manton, Caroline's husband, told police officers that she had left him after an argument and had gone to live in Hampstead, North London. He claimed not to know her new address.

Manton, a driver for the fire service, produced a letter he said had been written to him by his wife. However, detectives were becoming suspicious and asked him for a sample of his own handwriting. Expert analysis proved that he had written the letter, the real giveaway being his constant misspelling of "Hampstead" as "Hamstead."

Police dusted the house looking for fingerprints to compare with those belonging to the body, but found that their suspect had wiped all the surfaces clean.

SEARCH FOR PRINTS

Detectives commented that Manton must have been a reader of detective stories. He had certainly gone to great lengths to make sure that no fingerprints belonging to his absent wife were left anywhere in the house.

After several days of searching, Frederick Cherrill, Scotland Yard's top fingerprint expert at the time, found one solitary thumbprint on a pickle jar at the very back of the kitchen cupboard.

The print was matched to the thumbprint on the left hand of the body and police knew they had identified Mrs. Caroline Manton.

Shortly afterwards, Horace "Bertie" Manton confessed to killing his wife. They had argued and he had struck her with a heavy wooden stool in the kitchen. Placing her body in a sack, he had then taken it on the handlebars of his bike and dumped it in the river.

Worried that someone might spot that his wife had "left for Hampstead" without her coat in the middle of winter, he cut it to shreds and took it to the local dump. Manton was found guilty at Bedford Assizes and sent to Parkhurst prison.

The Luton Sack Murder illustrates how the smallest of clues can lead to a murderer's capture or his escape. If Detective Chief Inspector Chapman had not ordered his men to perform such a meticulous search of local dumping areas, the body would never have been identified.

On the other hand, of course, Mr. Manton was also the architect of his own downfall. If he had wiped the very last thumbprint off the pickle jar in the kitchen cupboard, police would have been unable to confirm the body as being his wife's.

It might seem to be the smallest of giveaways, but it was enough to send Manton to jail for the rest of his life.

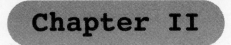

Chapter II

Every contact leaves a trace

Probably the single most important principle in detective work is Edmund Locard's statement that "Every contact leaves a trace."

Locard was a French criminologist who had been a great reader of Sherlock Holmes stories in his youth. Some of the fictional detective's genius may have rubbed off, because Locard went on to become one of the founding fathers of modern forensic science – the branch of science that collects and analyzes evidence for later use in a court of law.

THE EXCHANGE THEORY

Forensic scientists visit the scene of a crime to learn all that they can about the crime itself and who might have committed it. Often there are no human witnesses. However, "Every contact leaves a trace" refers to the many forensic clues that may link a murderer to his or her victim. Simply put, a criminal will always take something away from the scene of his or her crime and will always leave something behind.

Anything touched by a criminal will record his or her fingerprints. Any sweat or saliva left at the scene will enable scientists to produce a DNA profile. Clothes may leave behind tiny fibers which can later be matched to those worn by a certain suspect. A car will leave tire tracks behind. Even a single hair that falls from his or her head may, in expert hands, be used to prove guilt.

The reverse is also true. Fibers, hairs, tiny shards of shattered glass originating at the scene may attach themselves to the criminal while he or she is there.

Clues like these are called trace evidence. Although invisible to the naked eye and usually unnoticed by the criminal, they have resulted in the successful solution of thousands of criminal investigations.

FIRST FINGERPRINT CASE

Today, fingerprints are the best known type of forensic evidence in the world. Fingerprint patterns are made up of "loops," "arches," and "whorls" and no two people in the world have the same combination.

The first crime ever solved by fingerprinting was in 1892 by Police Inspector Álvarez from Buenos Aires, Argentina.

Inspector Álvarez was assigned to a double murder investigation in the small village of Necochea. Two people had been discovered murdered in the their hut and the case was proving too difficult for local police to solve. There was only one suspect for the murders, a farmer called Velásquez, but he refused to confess even when put under extreme pressure.

Álvarez visited the scene of the crime and as he looked around the hut, he noticed a thumbprint in blood on the door.

MARK OF A KILLER

Although fingerprinting as a means of solving crimes was unheard of, Inspector Álvarez had read that every person has a unique set of fingerprints and he realized that the bloody thumbprint could be a vital clue that should be saved as evidence.

But how could he save the solitary thumbprint? He had no method of "lifting" the print or otherwise recording it. The solution was obvious. Borrowing a saw, he cut the door away from its frame and took it back to police headquarters with him.

Inspector Álvarez soon began to suspect the owner of the shack and summoned twenty-five-year-old Francesca Rojas to his office. He asked her for her thumbprint, which he compared with the one on the door. Even though he was not an expert, Álvarez could tell that they were an exact match.

Faced with this strange new kind of evidence, Francesca Rojas confessed. Her murder conviction made history, as the first in the world to be based on fingerprint evidence.

MURDER IN DEPTFORD

The first British murder solved by fingerprint evidence was the March 1905 killing of seventy-year-old Thomas Farrow and his wife in Deptford High Street in London.

Someone had broken into Farrow's paint shop to rob it and had killed the Farrows in the process. Chief Inspector Fox of London's Scotland Yard took charge of the enquiry and quickly noticed a thumbprint inside the now empty cash box. The victims' fingerprints were taken along with those of everyone who worked in the shop but none were a match.

Police reasoned that the print must therefore belong to the killer. After more local enquiries were made, two brothers and well known petty crooks, Alfred and Albert Stratton, were picked up a few days later.

The thumbprint on Alfred's right hand was a perfect match for a print found on the small cash box where the Farrows kept their takings.

There was no other evidence or witnesses, but after much thought, the jury at their Old Bailey trial decided the thumbprint was enough evidence to find them guilty. The two brothers were hanged together on May 23, 1905.

MODERN FINGERPRINTING TECHNIQUES

Police scientists classify fingerprints into three different categories.

- *Visible prints* – left if the suspect has dirt, blood, or ink on his or her hands.
- *Plastic prints* – such as an impression of a fingerprint in paint, glue, chocolate, or any sticky surface.
- *Latent prints* – normal fingerprints that have been left by the oil and sweat on human hands and are invisible to the naked eye.

Fingerprints can be recorded in a variety of ways. A forensic scientist may dust for prints with a fine white powder and then use a piece of transparent tape to lift them from the surface they are on. If the prints are on a moveable object the whole thing may be taken away and the prints removed in the laboratory.

Forensic scientists can lift prints from surfaces as diverse as glass, plastic, wood, paper, and even bricks and stonework.

When the fingerprints have been recovered, they can be checked against the prints of known criminals associated with that particular type of crime.

The current FBI database of fingerprints contains over 200 million different prints, all available for computer comparison with those rushed in from a crime scene.

THE BENSON CAR BOMB

Fingerprints can sometimes be found in the strangest places.

When police were called to the Benson family home in Naples, Florida on July 9, 1985, they arrived to find a scene of devastation. The Bensons were about to drive off in their family car when it had suddenly erupted in a deadly explosion.

Two family members were killed, and one was seriously injured. Only Steve Benson escaped unhurt as he was fetching something from the house when the car exploded.

Police examined the wreckage and found that two metal tubes stuffed with explosives had been hidden in the car and had been set off by remote control as the family were about to drive away.

Detectives began looking for people with a grudge against the wealthy family or someone pursuing a business vendetta. The burned and charred fragments of the explosive device were taken to a forensics lab and subjected to the most intense examination.

Inside one of the bomb casings the scientists made a surprising discovery – a partial palm print of the man who had built and triggered the bomb.

When police compared it with the palm print of the only uninjured member of the family it was a perfect match. Steven Benson had blown up his own family. His motive was that he had found out that he was about to be cut out of his mother's will.

One moment of carelessness when he was making the explosive devices was enough to leave all the evidence that the police needed. Steven was sent to jail for a total of fifty years.

ON THE ROAD

If the criminal uses a car, the clues left behind can be just as valuable as fingerprints. Thomas Allaway was executed for murder in 1922, largely due to the tire-tracks found near his victim's body.

When Bournemouth police arrived at the crime scene where a woman's body had been discovered, they quickly noticed a set of rather distinctive tire-tracks made by the wheels of a car. Experts identified them as having been made by a Dunlop Magnum tire.

The seaside town of Bournemouth in 1922 had comparatively few cars of any description to check and the police soon had a suspect, Thomas Allaway, an ex-soldier now working as a chauffeur.

Samples of Allaway's handwriting were found to match with the handwriting on a telegram sent to the victim inviting her to come to Bournemouth earlier on the day of her death.

Allaway could only provide a weak alibi for the time of the murder and was found guilty when his case came to trial.

BITE-MARKS

Everyone's teeth are different so a bite-mark left at a crime scene can be a real help to police. Although it may sound unlikely, bite-marks are left behind by suspects more often than you might expect.

During any kind of attack or fight, people often resort to using their teeth. On other occasions, such as during a burglary, the criminal may actually pause to eat something at the scene.

One murderer from Essex was identified on the basis of a half-eaten pear that he abandoned by the side of his victim's body. American serial killer Ted Bundy was convicted on evidence largely backed up by the teeth marks that he made on one of his victims.

MANCHESTER MURDER

In one recent British case, the bite-marks of a dog became important evidence.

Officers rushed to the Manchester home of John Yates on April 27, 1996, only to find him lying in his doorway dead from a stab wound. A next-door neighbor had alerted police after hearing what sounded like a fight.

Inside the house, police located John's dog, Zac, who had also been attacked. A traumatized Zac, a large but friendly Alsatian with a long drooping tongue, was taken to the vet's where his injuries were treated.

Detectives found a letter in John's pocket which gave them a lead to start their investigation. A man called Christopher Allen soon became their main suspect and it was believed that he and the victim may have argued over a woman.

A taxi driver came forward to say that he had driven Christopher Allen to John's house on the night of the murder and then returned to the area later to pick him up again.

Forensic scientists examined the back seat of the taxi driver's cab, but could find no incriminating evidence.

CANINE WITNESS

One observant detective noticed that their suspect, Allen, had odd puncture wounds on his wrists. Allen tried to pass the injuries off as the result of an accident in the plastics factory where he worked. Having checked and found no record of an accident, detectives realized that maybe the wounds were from Zac, made as he tried to protect his master.

Detectives called Zac's new owner and arranged for him to visit the vet again. This time Zac was given an anesthetic and, while he was asleep, a plaster cast of his teeth was taken.

At Christopher Allen's trial in June 1997, the jury were shown how the plaster casts of Zac's teeth were a perfect match for the injuries on Allen's wrists. It was enough proof for the jury to send Allen to prison for life.

THE BUTTON AND THE BADGE

As well as trace evidence like fingerprints and tire tracks, killers often leave other items at the crime scene – items that turn out to be just as incriminating.

The body of Nellie Trew was found one cold morning on Eltham Common, South London in February 1918. Keen-eyed detectives searching the area around the body found a military badge and a button with a piece of wire threaded through it.

The distinctive badge was from a Leicestershire Army Regiment and, at the request of police anxious to trace its owner, was given much publicity in newspapers. A worker in a factory in Oxford Street, London realized that co-worker David Greenwood no longer had his badge, identical to the one the police had found.

When detectives questioned Greenwood he claimed to have sold his badge to a stranger on a train – a rather weak story that only made the police suspect him more. Greenwood lived in Eltham less than 100 yards from where the body was found.

Police asked to examine Greenwood's coat and discovered that all the buttons were missing. Presumably he had removed those remaining to prevent police comparing them with the button they had found near the body.

The clinching piece of evidence turned out not to be the button, however, but the piece of wire attached to it. The Oxford Street factory where Greenwood worked used exactly the same kind of wire on its production line. Greenwood was found guilty and sent to prison for life.

EXPERT WITNESSES

Forensic evidence usually relies on the courtroom testimony of expert witnesses, scientists called in by the police to examine the technical details of the crime scene. But, of course, it is not just the prosecution that makes use of experts. They are often called for the defense as well – leaving the judge and jury to decide who has the better argument.

Hair left at the crime scene is not as valuable to detectives as blood or fingerprints, but a sample of hair can give an indication of the suspect's age, sex, and ethic origin. Hair evidence can be very useful in proving that a suspect did have contact with a certain person or victim.

GUN ALLEY MURDER

The case of the Gun Alley Murder in Melbourne, Australia began on New Year's Eve, 1921. The body of a young woman had been dumped in a small alley near a busy part of the city.

Police suspicions focused on the owner of a local bar, Colin Ross, who witnesses remembered had been talking to the same red-headed woman at a nearby wine bar. Ross seemed very anxious to assist the police in any way he could. In fact, he was a little too eager, volunteering important details of the murder that had not been made public yet.

Officers searched Ross's home and, although most of the house had been thoroughly cleaned just recently, they did find several strands of long red hair on a blanket.

An analysis of the hair was carried out by a well respected forensic scientist, Dr. Charles Taylor. He found that the hair from the house matched the victim's and Ross was sent for trial. However, the story does not end there.

The defense lawyer knew that much of the police's case against Ross depended on the matching hair evidence. The defense then discovered that witnesses remembered another woman with long hair in the bar that night. They challenged Dr. Taylor to tell the difference between a sample of her hair and the victim's.

If Dr. Taylor failed to tell them apart then the police

knew their carefully constructed case would simply collapse.

Dr. Taylor worked hard and fast and was able to prove to the satisfaction of the jury that the hair from Ross's home was from the victim and not the other visitor to the bar. Ross was convicted and executed a few months later.

LOTTERY KIDNAPING

Some trace evidence used to solve crimes is just plain bizarre. In another Australian case, this time a kidnaping and murder, the killers were caught thanks to the evidence of two trees.

A few weeks after Basil and Freda Thorne won the Australian lottery their joy turned to horror when their son Graeme was kidnaped from near their Sydney home on July 7, 1960.

A ransom phonecall demanded $25,000 for his safe return. However, police allowed news to leak to the newspapers and the glare of publicity scared the kidnapers. Six weeks later, the kidnap victim was found dead.

The police had very little to go on. The whole country knew of the couple's lottery win thanks to the publicity they had received at the time, and almost anyone could have thought up the kidnap plot.

Careful examination of the body revealed plant spores from two distinct types of cypress trees. Botanical experts told police that it was extremely unusual to find both these types of tree growing in the same place.

MOST WANTED TREES

It was not much of a clue, but it was all the police had to start the investigation. For probably the first and only time in the history of crime detection, the police launched a "tree hunt" and searched for the improbable pairing.

They finally found the two types of tree together in the

garden of a house in Clontarf, about one mile from where the body had been found. Police knew they were on the right track when they found out that the couple who had been renting the house, Stephen and Megda Bradley, had mysteriously taken flight on the exact same day of the kidnaping.

Stephen Bradley (real name Istuan Baranyay) and his wife were arrested on board the passenger liner *Himalaya* as they sailed towards a new life in England. Stephen Bradley confessed to the kidnaping and was sentenced to life imprisonment, his capture thanks to the trace evidence of two trees.

Chapter III

Profiling – inside the mind of a killer

Most murders are committed by people who know their victims. They have a motive (often a very simple one) and they have the opportunity to commit the crime. However there is a different kind of murderer – one who has no connection whatsoever to his or her victim: the serial killer.

The most notorious criminals from history have all been serial killers – Jack the Ripper, the Son of Sam, Ted Bundy, Fred West, and the Yorkshire Ripper.

Serial killers are very difficult to catch because rather than murdering one particular person for a specific reason, they strike at randomly chosen targets with no other motive than the pleasure of killing.

With no connection between killer and victim, police are often at a loss as to where

28

to begin their investigation. It is in cases like these that detectives now turn to the technique of psychological profiling.

THE ART OF PROFILING

When an individual commits a series of murders or attacks, the crimes themselves can often give many pointers to the sort of person that is committing them. The technique of analyzing serial crime to learn things about the criminal is called psychological profiling.

Profilers like Britain's David Canter, who is Professor of Psychology at Liverpool University, believe that a criminal will always leave evidence of his or her personality behind through his or her actions and behavior. What psychological profiling does is to look at a number of murders or other attacks and ask the question, "What kind of person would do this?"

A psychological profile is built up by looking at the similarities in the crimes, with clues such as the method of murder, how the bodies were disposed of, and whether the victims had anything in common, as well as geographical and time factors like the time gaps between each of the attacks.

A person would not be found guilty in a court of law based solely upon a psychological profile. Profiling is used to help catch a criminal, but solid forensic evidence or a confession are needed to take the case to court.

HUNTING THE MAD BOMBER

The first psychological profile ever used in a police investigation was created by Dr. James Brussel in 1957. Dr. Brussel was a leading psychiatrist who worked for New York State's Mental Health department.

The police asked Dr. Brussel to try to assist them in their hunt for the "Mad Bomber" – an unknown man who had been terrorizing the city of New York for sixteen years by leaving home-made bombs in public places.

Detectives knew that the Mad Bomber was pursuing a one-man vendetta against a company called Consolidated Edison although they had no idea of his identity.

As a psychiatrist, Dr. Brussel already knew that he could study a man's mind and make reasonably accurate predictions about how that person would behave. Dr. Brussel's great leap was to reason that he could also do the reverse. He could look at a man's behavior (in the case of the Mad Bomber his crimes) and make deductions about his character and therefore his identity.

THE BIRTH OF PROFILING

Dr. Brussel went through the police's case file on the bomber and drew the following conclusions:

- the bomber was male – because most bombers are men;
- he was aged between forty and fifty – based on his paranoid state of mind;
- he had an obsessively neat personality – based on the handwriting in letters sent to the police;
- he was from a family that had immigrated to New York from Europe – based on the standard of English in the letters;
- his family were probably from Eastern Europe because that was where bombs were most often used as a protest at the time.

Altogether Dr. Brussel's profile ran to seventeen major points about the bomber, and police studied it carefully. Soon afterwards the bomber gave himself away through writing one letter too many to the police and was arrested. His name was George Metesky, and he was a male, middle-aged, neatly dressed, paranoid, son of an immigrant from Poland.

Dr. Brussel's profile of the bomber was an exact match of George Metesky in thirteen out of the seventeen categories.

Metesky had not been caught because of that first profile, but when its astonishing accuracy was revealed the newspapers of the time called Dr. Brussel "the Sherlock Holmes of the couch." Detectives were alerted to the potential value of Brussel's approach to serial crime.

Dr. Brussel was later brought in to help with the pursuit of a killer known as the Boston Strangler who murdered thirteen victims in 1962–63. Again, Brussel's psychological profile was uncannily accurate in describing Albert de Salvo – the man eventually found to be responsible.

THE FBI AND SERIAL KILLERS

During the 1970s and 1980s police forces noticed an alarming rise in seemingly random killings where there is no connection between a murderer and his or her victim.

FBI Special Agent Robert Ressler is often credited with the invention of the term "serial killer" which was quickly taken up by both the media and fiction writers. To count as a serial killer, the minimum FBI qualification is at least three separate killings at different times.

America leads the world in serial killers in terms of both famous names and sheer numbers. Luckily it also leads the way in catching them.

When agents at the FBI's National Training Academy began to look into the problem, their first step was to produce personality profiles for over two dozen serial killers already in custody. This involved agents conducting many long interviews with murderers in their prison cells.

The FBI's Behavioral Science Unit was formed to act as a pool for cutting-edge research and information about profiling. A part of the FBI Academy in Quantico, Virginia, the unit is housed in an old nuclear bomb shelter with no windows or natural light. It is staffed by FBI Special Agents and veteran police officers with degrees in either psychology or criminology.

Law-enforcement experts estimate that at any one time there are between thirty-five and fifty serial killers loose and active in the United States. Sadly, police expect this alarming figure to rise rather than fall. The good news, however, is that most serial killers are extremely predictable in their actions making profiling a very powerful tool against them.

Author and profiling expert Gary King says that once people become serial killers "their pattern of behavior rarely changes from crime to crime."

When the FBI's Behavioral Science Unit is asked to assist on a case they do not ask for a list of suspects to study. Their interest is in the exact details of the crimes and how they were committed. Their work, which is also called "offender profiling," is to draw conclusions as to what kind of suspect the police should be looking for.

THE COMPUTER PROFILER

The FBI's Behavioral Science Unit is asked for assistance on over 1,000 cases from around the world every single year. With that kind of workload it is just as well that some types of profiling can be performed by computer.

"Profiler" is a computer program which analyzes the details of crimes and creates a profile of the assailant by referring to pre-programmed rules. When it was first created, "Profiler" had 150 of these rules about the behavior of serial criminals. Today this number has doubled to more than 300.

A FBI agent inputs details about the crimes and the "Profiler" program sorts through this material in accordance with its 300 rules.

The profile produced suggests the attacker's age, race, whether single or married, intelligence, his or her likely type of employment, personality traits, possible hobbies, and a general description. Other items — such as whether the killer probably lives in the area of the attacks — will also be included.

After the computer has finished its work, its findings are always checked and re-examined by a human profiler who may give the results a new focus or direction. This is because profiling is by no means an exact science.

Human insight and the profiler's "gut instinct" also play important roles in the creation of an accurate profile. The art of profiling has been described as a mixture of craft, experience, and intelligence.

THE CAMPSITE MURDERS

One of the very first cases to be profiled by the FBI's unit were the murder of two holiday-makers near a woodland campsite in Montana USA in 1974. The local police reasoned that the killer was probably a local person, but they had already questioned everyone they considered likely and had come up with no obvious suspects.

The profile produced by the unit described the killer as a young white male, quiet and unassuming. He would live near to the campsite and had probably kept some item belonging to the victims as a memento of his crimes. The profile also suggested that he might well call a relative of one of the victims to boast that he was still free.

The profile's description fitted a man called David Meirhofer, but the police had no evidence against him until one of the victim's families did receive a phone call from the killer. At the insistence of the FBI, both families had had a tape recorder set up on the phone line and the call was taped.

The voice was later identified as belonging to David Meirhofer and this was enough for police to be able to get a search warrant for his home. Inside the police found evidence that directly linked him to the killings. He confessed to the murders a short time later, as well as to two other killings that detectives had not even linked him with.

The technique of profiling had caught its first serial killer.

THE RAILWAY KILLER

The first British serial killer to be caught by profiling was John Duffy, commonly known as the Railway Killer because many of his attacks took place near or on railway lines. He was arrested after his name was highlighted by a profile produced by England's Professor David Canter, then of Surrey University.

Professor Canter was first approached by detectives from London's Scotland Yard in 1985. The detectives were investigating a series of twenty-five attacks and three murders in the Greater London area, and they had heard about the early work of the FBI's Behavioral Science Unit. They wanted to know if Professor Canter could create a similar system for them.

Two detectives worked with Professor Canter and together

they used a computer to search through the many crime files for what Professor Canter describes as "The essence of the offender, his character or personality."

Having analyzed the crimes, Professor Canter wrote his first ever profile describing the assailant as:

- living in the immediate area of the first three attacks;
- living with a partner but no children;
- in his late twenties;
- being right-handed, with fair hair and 5′ 9″ in height;
- having a skilled job;
- probably quiet: keeps to himself, but has one or two close male friends;
- has a good working knowledge of the Greater London railway system.

NEEDLE IN A HAYSTACK

Professor Canter gave his profile to the detectives in charge of the case who already had a computer-generated list of the 2,000 most likely suspects. They ran the profile against the list of suspects and one name was a perfect match for the profile – John Duffy.

Duffy was put under police surveillance and his odd behavior aroused suspicions even further. He was arrested on November 23, 1986 and a search of his house revealed strong forensic evidence (hairs and fibers) linking him to the murders.

In chapter two we looked at the well-known principle of forensic science formulated by Edmond Locard that "every contact leaves a trace." Although Locard was referring to physical evidence, Professor Canter suggests that "there is also a more subtle meaning . . . the contact that an attacker has with his victim leaves behind a trace of the sort of person he is."

In the case of the Railway Killer those traces of his personality were enough to pick him out of a list of 2,000 other suspects.

STALKING SERIAL KILLERS

Another of the UK's top profilers, Paul Britton, compares the art of profiling to putting together a jigsaw puzzle. He says, "at the start of every investigation I ask myself four questions. What happened? How did it happen? Who was the victim? And why did it happen?"

Only when Britton is confident that he has the answers does he turn his attention to the most important question: "Who was responsible?"

Britton has helped police in more than 100 serious cases. When profiling a criminal, he tries to get right inside his head, attempting to "see the world through his eyes and to hear the sounds he hears."

Psychological profiling was quickly seized upon by writers of detective stories and thrillers. A deadly cat-and-mouse game between profiler and killer has now become a popular theme in books, TV, and film.

Thomas Harris's chilling novels *Red Dragon* and *The Silence of the Lambs* were among the first to include profiling. The idea has also been used by producer Chris Carter in his TV series *Millennium* and *The X-Files*. Indeed some of *The X-Files'* best episodes such as "Grotesque" and "Paperhearts" have been based on profiles.

JACK THE RIPPER

Profiling has even been applied to serial killers of the past. When the technique first received media attention in the late 1980s there were several attempts (including one involving FBI agents) to use post-dated profiling to solve one of the greatest mysteries of modern crime – the identity of Jack the Ripper.

The Ripper murders took place in the Whitechapel area of east London in the fall of 1888. Although no forensic evidence survives, it is still possible to produce at least a preliminary profile based on the geographic locations of the victims, the timings of the five murders, and the choice of victim.

Professor Canter is among those who have looked at the case and he suggests (as others have done) that if the killer were living in Whitechapel then the murders were probably distributed in an area (roughly a circle) around his home or place of lodging.

Many names have been put forward over the years for the real identity of Jack the Ripper, including those of members of the Royal family and of a leading doctor of the time. Of all the many possible Ripper suspects, Professor Canter's profile points the finger at one in particular – Aaron Kosminski, a barber living in the middle of the murder area. Shortly after the murders, Kosminski went mad and later died in a mental asylum.

THE PROFILING NET

Of course, psychological profiling is a far from perfect technique. This chapter has focused on some of its successes, but there have also been failures – cases where the profile was incomplete or inaccurate, and others where it was just plain wrong. Occasionally investigations have even been sent in the wrong direction by a bad profile and valuable police time has been wasted.

Perhaps as a result of it being over-hyped and hailed as a miracle when it first emerged, profiling has its fair share of critics. However, balanced by common sense and given a proper role within a police investigation, profiling can offer important insights into the type of suspect that police should concentrate their efforts on.

Perhaps psychological profiling represents the ultimate dead giveaway, as a criminal's own personality allows the police to discover his or her identity, leading to his or her arrest.

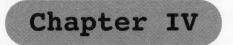

Chapter IV

Psychics

If identifying a killer through psychological profiling seems amazing, then consider the individuals who claim they are able to do the same thing using special powers – psychic detectives.

Many police forces all over the world have used the help of psychics. A few psychics like Noreen Renier, who predicted the attempted assassination of President Ronald Reagan, have even given lectures at the FBI Academy in Quantico.

Skeptics may dispute the existence of their powers, but that does not stop detectives asking psychics for help when they run out of other options.

People have been putting questions to psychics in one form or another for hundreds, if not thousands, of years.

In ancient times, each tribe would have its own wise man or Shaman who would use his special powers to seek answers to questions and obtain knowledge that was unavailable to normal men.

During medieval times, the victim of a crime would consult a "cunning man." Each local village would have its own cunning man who used various supernatural or other-worldly methods to find the guilty party responsible for a crime.

THE DIVINING-ROD DETECTIVE

Frenchman Jacques Aymar was probably the world's first recognizable psychic detective. In the summer of 1692, a case involving the robbery and murder of a wine merchant made him famous across Europe.

A wine merchant and his wife had been robbed and murdered in the town of Lyons in France. Local police were left with very few clues to help them catch the killers. The public were outraged by the crime and were clamoring for the police to make an arrest.

When Jacques Aymar approached officials offering them his help, police reasoned that they had little to lose.

Aymar made use of a divining rod to detect that the crime had been committed by three people. He then used the rod

to follow their trail like a bloodhound. Aymar followed the scent all the way to a nearby prison where he picked a man from a line-up of a dozen prisoners.

It seemed that since committing the murders, the killer had fallen foul of the law on some other charge. The man was taken back to Lyons, where he told them the names of the other men involved in the attack, and made a full confession that included details of the crimes only known to the police.

Soon afterwards, Aymar was given a formal role with the police department and he helped them in several other investigations.

THE BODY IN THE BASEMENT

The first case in the modern age of psychic detection involved Kate and Margaret Fox, and their home in Hydesville, New York.

During a 1848 spirit-rapping (in which a spirit sounds one rap on the table for "no," two raps for "yes") they were told of a murder that had taken place in their own home. A "spirit" claiming to be a travelling peddler said that he had been robbed and murdered by an individual with the initials "C.R.," and that his body had been buried in the cellar of the house.

Records showed that the house had once been occupied by a man named Charles Rosana. This was enough to make the excited sisters hire workmen to dig up the cellar floor. The searchers found a skull fragment from a human head along with some other bones.

Charles Rosana, who was now living happily in New York, was outraged that he should be linked with an allegation of murder, and without further evidence the investigation stopped there.

Over fifty years later, the new owners of the house were

having some building work carried out. The work revealed a hidden cavity in a wall containing the rest of a male skeleton, and on the floor next to it was a small tin box such as was used by peddlers.

THE CASE OF THE DISAPPEARING DETECTIVE STORY WRITER

In 1926 a strange disappearance occurred that brought together two of the world's greatest ever detective writers – Agatha Christie and Arthur Conan Doyle.

Conan Doyle was the creator of Sherlock Holmes, but despite being the "father" of the ever-logical Baker Street detective, Conan Doyle was a great believer in psychics and their powers. He once said he thought that psychic detectives would become the single most important tool of crime-detection in the future.

Conan Doyle was asked to help when fellow novelist Agatha Christie went missing under mysterious circumstances in December 1926. Mrs. Christie's car was found abandoned in Surrey and despite a massive police search, no further trace of her could be found.

MURDER MOST FOUL?

Had the most famous murder writer in the world herself been murdered? Many people including most of the national newspapers thought that she had.

Conan Doyle took a glove belonging to Mrs. Christie to a psychic to obtain a reading. The psychic held the glove (without knowing to whom it belonged) and told Conan Doyle that the owner was not dead but was hiding somewhere in a spa town, and that he would receive news of that person next Wednesday.

When Wednesday arrived and Conan Doyle looked at the front page of his morning newspaper, he saw that Mrs. Christie had indeed been found. Alive and allegedly suffering from amnesia, she had been staying in the Hydropathic Hotel in Harrogate for the previous eleven days.

Conan Doyle recorded that he was well pleased with the psychic's information and continued to make similar consultations for the rest of his life.

MURDERS AT THE FARM

An outstanding example of a psychic detective helping to solve a case was the multiple murders at Mannville near Edmonton in Canada.

Two members of the Booher family and two of the farm workers were found shot to death at the family farm in July 1928. It soon became clear that detectives were making little progress with the case. They had no suspects, no motive for the killings, and could not even find the .303 rifle that was the murder weapon.

Finally, the man leading the investigation, Inspector William Hancock, decided to enlist the help of someone with rather special talents. He turned to Maximilian Langsner, who had recently used his famed psychic powers to solve a jewelry robbery in Vancouver when had helped police recover stolen gems.

Langsner attended the inquest into the four deaths and shortly announced that in fact the terrible crime had been committed by family member Vernon Booher himself. The surprised detectives treated this information with skepticism but, undeterred, the psychic told the police that he would lead them to the murder weapon.

WEAPON HUNT

Next day, Langsner and a group of policemen went back to the farm. At first Langsner wandered around getting a sense of the location in much the same way that dowsers do. Soon, however, he identified a newly-dug mound of earth and told police to look there. Police quickly found a .303 rifle that had been hastily buried.

The man that Langsner had earlier identified as the killer, Vernon Booher, was taken into custody. With no evidence linking him to the gun itself, he could not be arrested and so detectives told him that it was for his own protection.

Maximilian Langsner travelled back to the jail as well and sat silently outside the man's cell. Booher repeatedly tried to strike up a conversation with Langsner, but Langsner ignored him and remained completely silent.

THE MISSING WITNESS

When Langsner finished his quiet vigil he told police details of how Booher had committed the murders, details he claimed to have "seen" in Booher's mind. The psychic also told detectives that somewhere in town there was a woman who was a key witness against Booher.

Langsner said she had spotted the suspect sneaking out of a church service to go and steal the gun he used for the murders. He could not name the woman, but he had seen what she looked like in Booher's mind and could give them a detailed description of her.

Mannville was a tiny country town and it did not take police long to track down the woman described. Her name was Erma Higgins and she had indeed seen Vernon Booher behaving suspiciously.

When Booher was confronted with both the recovered murder weapon and the statement of Erma Higgins, he confessed to the killings immediately. His detailed confession fitted exactly with the description of events given by Langsner. Vernon Booher was found guilty and was later hanged.

The Manville murders was the last time that Maximilian Langsner ever assisted police on a case. He spent the rest of his life in Alaska, studying the psychic and ESP talents of the local Inuit community.

MODERN PSYCHIC DETECTIVES

British psychic Nella Jones comes from gypsy descent and claims that she was always aware of her psychic abilities even in her childhood. When Nella was seven years old, she remembers predicting the death of a local woman about a week before it actually happened.

Nella's first involvement as a psychic detective began in 1970 when she was watching a television news report about a valuable painting, *The Guitar Player*, that had been stolen.

Suddenly, Nella began seeing a location in her head and sketched a map of Kenwood House where the painting had been taken from. She marked one particular point on the map with a cross.

Nella contacted the police who asked her to accompany them to the area. They found the spot identified by the cross on Nella's map, and there, lying on the ground, was an empty picture frame and the alarm system that had been supposed to protect it.

Nella told police that she felt that the painting was now hidden in a cemetery. A search of Highgate Cemetery found nothing, but interestingly, the painting was eventually recovered from The City of London Cemetery about ten miles to the east.

This kind of partial success is a common feature of cases involving psychic detectives. Good psychics produce information that is often impressive, but none of them are ever 100 percent accurate.

THE RIPPER PREMONITIONS

Since the Kenwood painting incident, Nella has been contacted by police forces from all around Britain many times and asked for help with their investigations. One of her most famous premonitions involved the British serial killer known as The Yorkshire Ripper. In the late 1970s, as the hunt for the killer stalking women in the north of England intensified, desperate police contacted several psychics.

Nella told police that she thought the man's name was Peter, that he had a beard, and that he spent his days driving a long-distance truck. When Peter Sutcliffe was arrested nearly two years after her predictions, Nella was proved correct.

Even more extraordinarily, when Nella gave her original predictions she also singled out the date of the next attack. She said it would be on either the 17th or 27th of November

(1980) and that the victim of the attack would have the initials "J.H."

Remarkably and tragically, on the 17th of November Peter Sutcliffe claimed his thirteenth and last victim. Her name was Jacqueline Hill.

Like many other psychics, Nella describes herself as tuning in to the information that she receives, as if it were being broadcast to her. With the Sutcliffe predictions, Nella felt a great sense of fear and evil as the picture unfolded in her mind.

Other psychics also feel as if the information is being broadcast to them from somewhere else. American psychic Dorothy Allison describes the sensation as "like pictures on a flickering TV screen."

THE RIGHT KIND OF CASE

Psychic detectives seem to have more success with certain kinds of crime than others. In cases involving missing people, kidnaping, or murder they seem to be more accurate, more often. Perhaps because it is easier for them to "tune in" when very strong and intense emotions are involved.

Top American psychic Greta Alexander was able to lead police officers to the body of missing Larry Dean over the phone, even though she was in a town 130 miles away from the actual scene of the investigation.

Dean had fallen into the Iroquois River near Watseka in Illinois, USA. He had been carried away by strong winter currents and could have been anywhere along the entire length of the river.

Police contacted Greta and she began to see images of where the body was located, again describing the process as being "like watching television inside my head. I become the antenna and I just pick up the picture."

Greta talked to police on a mobile phone and directed

them to the exact spot. The officers found the body of Larry Dean just where Greta said they would.

WORKING WITH PSYCHICS

While psychics can provide good and sometimes startlingly accurate information for police forces, they also have their fair share of misses.

Lorne Mason, a paranormal investigator who has made a study of police work with psychics, told me: "Police forces should not ignore psychics and refuse to work with them, but they should not rely solely on psychic information either. Their skills should be used like the specialist talents of any other outside expert. Any information they provide needs to be weighed up against common sense and taken in the overall context of the investigation."

A police force that does work with psychics needs to use them and their evidence very carefully. The testimony of a psychic is not admissible in a court of law, and an arrest resulting from psychic information needs to be backed up by solid everyday police work or it will not stand up in court.

MISSING

Police forces are not the only emergency service to have assistance from psychics. Ian Middleton and Steve Swindlehurst are two British men who owe their lives to a German dowser.

During a skiing holiday in the Bavarian Alps in Germany in February 1994, Ian and Steve travelled up the mountain in search of a particularly difficult ski run.

They began to ski down the run, but soon took a wrong turn and found themselves completely lost on the hostile slopes of the mountain. They tried to find their way back, but the routes they tried ended in sheer rock cliffs. To make things even worse, thick fog was closing in on the whole area.

When they failed to return to the village below, their friends alerted the Oberammergau Mountain Rescue service who immediately sent out teams of searchers. By this time, it was getting dark and Ian and Steve had wandered into an area of thick forest.

The search parties could not find them on the slopes and as night fell they returned to the village empty-handed.

The two men were trapped on the mountain where the nighttime temperature would fall to minus 20° – easily enough to stop their hearts beating and kill them.

THE OLD MAN OF THE MOUNTAINS

Enter seventy-year-old Georg Horak. Georg had lived in the village all his life, and knew the slopes of the surrounding mountains better than almost anyone else. When he heard about the lost men, he went straight to his home to consult his divining rod.

He held the rod over a detailed map of the mountain, moving it across the map slowly. Georg was sure that he could sense the "lines of power" on the mountain slopes and he hoped that these would tell him the location of the men.

Georg found the rod had a strong reaction to one specific location and he became sure that the men were there. He felt that he could sense the danger that the men were in and he passed on the location to the Rescue Service.

They trusted Georg and for the second time that night the search teams headed up the mountain. They followed Georg's instructions and began to search an area of thick forest. The search team's flashlights soon picked out the faces of the two very cold, but very happy, skiers.

The divining skills of Georg Horak had saved their lives. Another few hours on the mountain and Ian and Steven would certainly have been dead.

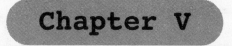

Chapter V

Great mistakes

Committing the perfect crime and getting away scot-free is a difficult task. What with police detectives, forensic scientists, psychological profilers, and psychics on their trail, you might think that criminals would have a tough enough time already.

Some lawbreakers, however, can't help making things even harder for themselves.

As an example, consider the case of John Roberts from Pennsylvania, USA. Roberts spent over a week planning a bank robbery in the summer of 1994. He took care to work out what kind of mask he would wear, how much money he could carry, and what his best getaway route would be.

When he finally put his plan into action, the raid went like clockwork, and bank staff filled up his bag until it was brimming with used cash. Roberts made staff and customers lie on the floor, then left the building before police arrived.

Having made sure that he was not being followed, Roberts slipped back to his apartment and paused to count the money before skipping town for good.

Within minutes there was a knock at the door and Roberts found himself confronted by half a dozen police officers – who promptly arrested him.

Roberts wondered how they had tracked him down so very quickly. Had someone recognized him under his mask?

Or had he been followed from the bank after all? Police pointed to his jacket, now lying across the back of a chair, and Roberts realized his mistake.

He had worn his favorite jacket for the robbery as he did for all important occasions. Embroidered across its back, in large letters, was his name "John Edward Roberts."

THE CURIOUS CASE OF THE COUNTLESS CLUES

Some criminals make a little more effort though, and some even try to help police by pointing them in the direction of another person altogether.

When police arrived at a murder scene in the Borough of Queens, New York in July 1937, they immediately became hopeful of finding the killer.

Police had been called to a patch of waste ground when neighbors heard a woman's screams coming from the area. Searching the site, they found the body of twenty-year-old Mrs. Phennie Perry who had been killed with a blow to the head.

Mrs. Perry seemed to have put up quite a struggle against her attacker, because lying scattered around her were several items that seemed to offer the police hope of catching her killer. There was a man's left shoe (with a hole in its sole) and a collection of letters addressed to a Mr. Ulysses Palm, many stained with blood from the attack.

Obviously the police's first task was to pay a visit to Mr. Palm's house. Mr. Palm was out as police began their search, but detectives were delighted to find a right shoe that was the partner of the one found at the murder scene. Mud from the shoe was matched to the murder scene and police were sure they had their man.

Together with her husband, the victim had rented a room from Ulysses Palm. When Mrs. Perry's husband, Arthur Perry, told police that Mr. Palm had argued with and then threatened his wife, it seemed an open and shut case.

To prepare evidence for the court case, detectives had to check out Arthur Perry's story and when they did, they found it made no sense. At the exact time that Arthur Perry claimed he saw the argument between his wife and Ulysses Palm, several witnesses placed him over eight miles away in another town.

The detectives suddenly became suspicious. Searching his house, police found an unwashed pair of socks that were to prove Arthur Perry's undoing.

FORENSIC FRAME-UP

On one of the socks was a tell-tale mud print in exactly the same position as the hole in the shoe that police had found. Careful forensic work also revealed traces of human blood on the sock – and this was later found to be the same blood type as his wife's. Soil from the bottom of the shoe was also matched to the crime scene.

It was now clear to the investigating officers that Perry had attempted a frame-up.

Arthur Perry had worn the shoes to murder his wife, and

deliberately left one at the murder scene, along with letters that he knew would lead police to search Ulysses Palm's house. He then broke into the Palm residence and planted the other shoe where he hoped police would find it.

The first part of his plan had worked perfectly, and Ulysses Palm had been arrested. Perry had not expected detectives to be so diligent in checking out his story. He had used the shoes to frame Ulysses Palm, but had not realized that, if found, the pair of socks he had worn during the murder could do the same to him.

Like any villain in a classic episode of Peter Falk's *Columbo* series, he had not expected police to be so hard-working. His ingenious plan in ruins, Perry was electrocuted two years later.

THE MYTH OF FINGERPRINTS

If you're not going to plant fake evidence, then how about making sure you leave no evidence at all? Following the introduction of the FBI's fingerprint system in the 1930s, a gangster by the name of Robert Pitts had just that in mind when he had all his fingerprints removed.

Pitts reasoned that without fingerprints police would be unable to link him to the crimes he intended to carry out. Pitt knew that having his fingerprints removed by the surgeon's knife or dissolved by acid would not work – the same patterns just grow back again as the skin heals.

Falling under the category of "it seemed a good idea at the time," Pitts decided to try something else. He had his fingerprints surgically removed and then had a skin graft of neutral skin put on to the ends of his fingers. After the operation, he spent a painful two months with his arms in bandages while the flesh healed.

Where other criminals had failed, Pitts had now succeeded. He had no fingerprints. Although a good idea in theory, it didn't quite work out as well in practice.

Unfortunately, Pitts was the only man in the world with no fingerprints – a fact that rather made him stand out from the other four billion people on the planet. He was now more noticeable than ever.

Following an arrest in Texas, the man with no prints went to jail.

POWERS OF THE MIND

Sometimes it is a murderer's over-confidence or eagerness to be seen to help police that is his or her undoing. The Owen Etheridge murder case is not only an outstanding case of psychic detection, but also a classic example of a murderer trying too hard to cover his tracks.

When teenager Owen Etheridge walked into the building of his local radio station in Lompoc, California on April 7th, 1978, he was intending to help establish the final touch to his cover story. Instead, he ended up walking into a murder conviction.

Owen Etheridge had come to the radio station to talk to Dixie Yeterian, a psychic who had her own call-in show during which she tried to help troubled callers with their problems.

Earlier in that April day, Owen had called Dixie's program and had spoken to her on-air. The boy had seemed very worried and told Dixie how his father had gone away on a business trip and had not returned.

Dixie was often used by the local police to help with kid-nap and missing-person cases and she asked Owen to come down to the station to talk to her in person.

When the two of them were face to face, Owen explained once again how worried he was that his father seemed to have vanished off the face of the Earth.

Dixie had asked Owen to bring along something of his father's so she could hold it while she tried to get her psychic impressions. Owen handed over his father's watch, a special family keepsake.

A SURPRISING SOLUTION

As soon as Dixie touched the watch, images began flooding into her mind. She described what she was seeing as "like a movie being shown inside my head." Dixie found herself

"watching" an argument between Owen's father and some-one else. The yelling and shouting got worse and worse until it erupted into violence and the father was the victim of a gunshot.

The point of view of the movie changed, and for the first time Dixie saw the face of the person who had fired the gun: it was Owen Etheridge himself.

She then watched as Owen set about the task of covering up the killing and hiding the body. Dixie watched as Owen wrapped the body in a green sheet and then moved it across town before finally burying it on a patch of waste ground.

Dixie was shocked and wondered if the skinny seventeen-year-old in front of her could really have killed his own father. She needed time to think and, saying nothing about what she had "seen," she told Owen she would need to do another reading later.

The second reading was arranged for later the same day. As Dixie held the watch for the second time, she saw the same sequence of events unfold just as before. Now fearing for her own life, she told Owen nothing of what she suspect-ed and informed him that she had not been able to get a clear result.

CALLING IN THE POLICE

After Owen had left, Dixie called the local police station and spoke to homicide detective Mel Ramos.

Detective Ramos already knew Dixie, having already worked with her on several missing-person cases. He respected her talent as a psychic and listened carefully as she told him the whole story. Dixie asked him to look into it, say-ing that she was sure she was right about the killing.

Ramos trusted Dixie enough to start asking questions and headed over to Owen's home. The first thing that impressed the detective was that the layout of the house was just as Dixie had described it from her vision, although she had never physically been there.

Ramos began by questioning the boy as casually as possible, but the longer this went on the more edgy Owen seemed to get and the more suspicious Ramos became. Owen was taken into the police station for questioning during which Ramos decided to confront the boy directly with what Dixie had reported. The boy sat quietly for a moment, then surprised everyone by saying that he would take them to where the body was buried.

Dixie Yeterian had told Ramos that the body would be found "buried in the east of town, wrapped in a green sheet with a green cloth tied tightly around the neck." In actual fact the body was hidden on waste ground in the east of town, was wrapped in a green sheet and had a green cord (not cloth) tied tightly around the neck.

Ramos, who had seen Dixie help his police department on a number of occasions, described Dixie's solution to the Etheridge murder as "an outstanding case."

THE MAN WHO CAUGHT HIMSELF

Owen Etheridge had shot his father in a fit of rage and deeply regretted it afterwards. To escape being found out, Owen had immediately set about creating the perfect cover story. Trying to look like the dutiful son sick with worry, Owen had even rung a hotel where his father sometimes stayed on business to see if he was there. The telephone call was all part of the cover story in case police checked up on him.

Owen did not believe in the existence of psychic powers, and thought all psychics were frauds. Asking Dixie for help was supposed to be the final act of a son desperate to find his dad. Owen did not know that Dixie would see everything, including him pulling the trigger.

When Dixie Yeterian contacted the police, she was helping them solve a crime they were not even aware had been committed.

If Owen had not involved the psychic in his cover-up scheme, his father would have remained as one among thousands of missing people and Owen would have got away with his murder. He had not realized that going to a genuinely gifted psychic, like Dixie, was such a high-risk strategy.

Owen Etheridge was found guilty of murder and sentenced to life imprisonment.

A MAN'S BEST FRIEND?

Police don't always need the help of someone with psychic powers to track down a criminal of course. In one case from Sapporo in northern Japan a man was turned in by his best friend – his own dog.

A twenty-three-year-old man was walking his dog one evening when he spotted a brand new television set sitting in the back of a parked car.

The man tied his faithful dog to a nearby railing and smashed one of the car's windows to get inside.

The noise of the breaking glass alerted the owner who came running out of his house. The would-be thief had to flee into the night leaving his dog still tied to the metal railing.

When detectives arrived, they untied the dog, who walked calmly across town and straight back to its master's house. Police followed the unsuspecting canine snitch and promptly burst inside to arrest the man.

THE NOT-SO-PERFECT ALIBI

When Eric Laymon was arrested and charged with committing a drive-by shooting in New Orleans in March 1994, his mother immediately leapt to his defense.

She was furious at what she saw as an attempt to frame "my boy," and she called a press conference outside the main New Orleans police station to announce that "Eric couldn't possibly have been involved because at exactly ten thirty, when the drive-by shooting took place, he was over on the other side of town murdering someone else who owed us money."

The assembled crime reporters could hardly believe their ears as she concluded: "He shot him through the head. So I tell you again, my boy is innocent and I have the dead body to prove it."

Police were more than happy to drop the drive-by shooting and replace it with a murder charge. Detectives said that with a few more alibis like Mrs Laymon's, they could clear up crime in New Orleans very quickly.

Chapter VI

DNA-profiling

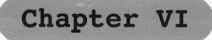

Until recently, fingerprints were the single most important forensic evidence found at crime scenes. But in the 1980s the face of crime-detection changed with the introduction of a brilliant new technique called DNA-profiling.

This vital breakthrough in forensic science was made by Dr. (now Professor) Alec Jeffreys in 1984 while working at Leicester University in the UK. DNA, which stands for deoxyribonucleic acid, is the substance which maps out the human body, tells it how to grow, and makes us what we are.

DNA is contained in all human cells and is a very complex molecule in the shape of a double helix. A person's height, hair color, and all other physical characteristics are decided by their DNA which is often called "the blueprint for life."

THE VITAL BREAKTHROUGH

Dr. Jeffreys had been working on research with proteins when he managed to isolate a length of DNA. It was the section which gives an individual his or her very own personal and unique characteristics.

Using a radioactive probe, Dr. Jeffreys managed to transfer DNA samples onto a piece of film where they could be seen more clearly. The result looked rather like the black and white lines on a supermarket bar code.

Dr. Jeffreys realized that, like fingerprints on a hand, no two people in the world – except identical twins – would have exactly the same DNA sequence. Even otherwise identical twins, however, do have different physical fingerprints.

DNA PROFILES

This new method of identifying suspects is of enormous value to the police.

DNA is contained in blood, skin tissue, saliva, sweat, and hair (as long as the root is still attached to it). New techniques now mean that a suspect's DNA can be extracted from substances such as ear wax, nasal mucus, and even flecks of dandruff.

Thanks to the constantly improving methods of forensic scientists, just touching a surface with your hand can leave enough material behind to produce a DNA profile.

This means that there are numerous possibilities at a crime scene for obtaining a DNA profile of the criminal. As soon as the police have a suspect, a blood sample can be taken from him or her and the two DNA profiles can be compared.

This is a stunning leap forward for crime-detection.

THE FIRST DNA MURDER CASE

The first time DNA-testing was used was in Britain in 1987 when it resulted in the capture of a double murderer –

although in a rather unexpected way.

Leicestershire police were running out of options to pursue in their hunt for the vicious killer of two local women. DNA-profiling had never been used in a criminal investigation before, but even so Detective Superintendent David Baker decided that it was the best and maybe the only way forward.

The police had a suspect, but when his DNA was compared with DNA from the crime scenes it was clear that he was innocent and he was released.

FIVE THOUSAND TESTS

Embarrassed Leicestershire detectives were now left without a suspect, but since a DNA profile had freed an innocent man, they reasoned that it could trap the guilty killer as well.

Faced with few other avenues to explore, they decided to launch the world's first DNA-based manhunt. Police announced that they would DNA-test all males in the local area between the ages of eighteen and thirty-five.

The whole process went on for many months and between January and August of 1987 over five thousand men were tested. Blood and saliva samples were taken from the test subjects and compared with DNA material found at the crime scene. However, none of the five thousand gave a positive result.

As the summer went on, more and more of the local population were gradually ruled out as suspects. The DNA-testing operation was very costly and by early fall the newspapers and other media were beginning to suggest that the whole idea was an expensive waste of time.

The police got the break they desperately needed when they learned that a man called Colin Pitchfork had persuaded a friend to take the DNA test for him. It emerged that Pitchfork had swapped the photograph in his passport for one of a work colleague, who then gave a blood sample in his place.

The police obviously wondered why the twenty-seven-year-old bakery worker was so keen to avoid taking the test? When detectives arrived to question Colin Pitchfork, he confessed to the murders almost immediately. Police took a blood sample and to their satisfaction found that his DNA was a perfect match with samples found at both murder scenes. DNA-testing had not caught him directly, but trying to avoid it had. He was sentenced to life imprisonment.

DNA GOES INTERNATIONAL

Tommie Lee Andrews had the distinction of being the first American criminal to be found guilty thanks to DNA evidence. In 1988 he was sent to prison for attacks on two women, largely on the basis of DNA samples. Police forces all around the globe were quick to realize that DNA-profiling was a major new weapon in their efforts against crime.

In the early days, obtaining a DNA profile was a costly and time-consuming business with results taking up to six weeks to come back from the lab.

More recently, however, Dr. Jeffreys made another major breakthrough in the field when he introduced a new system called Digital DNA-profiling. This technique is many times more sensitive than the old method, and also reduces the time taken to produce a profile from six weeks to forty -eight hours.

UNSOLVED MURDER

The new and recent advances in DNA-testing techniques have also enabled police to re-open some old crime files.

Barbara Mayo was hitchhiking from London to Yorkshire in October 1975 when she was picked up by an unknown person and killed. At the time of the murder, police launched a massive nationwide manhunt for the killer, but with no results.

Now, over two decades later, the Forensic Science Service have given the police new evidence that they hope will help finally solve the case.

Using the very latest techniques for extracting DNA, scientists have pro- duced a DNA profile of the killer from a tiny stain on material found at the original crime scene. The piece of clothing had been carefully stored since the crime. Only now has technology become so advanced as to allow a seemingly useless stain to yield such vital and telling evidence.

Somewhere out there is a killer who believes he has escaped justice, and although at the moment police don't have a suspect to check the DNA evidence against, when they do find a match they can be sure they have the right man.

Ben Gunn, Chief Constable of Cambridgeshire, UK, reasons that "it may well be good practice for all forces to revisit unsolved serious crimes to see if there is any evidence that might convert to a DNA profile."

A DATABASE OF KILLERS

The DNA profile of the Mayo killer can be used by police in several different ways. It can be compared with DNA profiles collected from other unsolved crime scenes, or it can even be matched to DNA of an offender already serving time in prison.

Nearly 200,000 DNA profiles of convicted and suspected criminals are held on computer at the Forensic Science Service in Birmingham, UK. Because the profiles are held on computer, they are available for checking in a matter of minutes. DNA profiles are so accurate that the chances of a match being made in error is now one in one billion.

In America, the FBI is in the process of spending millions of dollars to update its own DNA database to speed up the comparison of crime scene samples with DNA profiles already on record.

Police forces everywhere are convinced of one thing: DNA-profiling works. For example, in just six months during 1997 in Britain alone, DNA profiles were responsible for identifying criminals in 9 murder cases, 468 car crimes and nearly 4,000 burglaries.

BODY FOUND

Surprisingly, it is not just human DNA that can be used to catch killers.

On May 6, 1995, the body of Shirley Duguay was discovered buried in wild woodlands in Canada. She had been missing for months, during which time a blood-stained jacket had already been found at another site in the huge forest. The blood on the jacket matched Shirley's.

Police immediately arrested their prime suspect – her common-law husband Douglas Beamish. Beamish had a history of violence and, having already made various threats against her, he was the obvious suspect.

The blood-stained jacket had undoubtedly been worn by the murderer, but Beamish said the jacket was not his and detectives could not prove otherwise. It looked as if a guilty man was about to walk out of jail, because police lacked any hard evidence linking Beamish to the murder.

SNOWBALL

When forensic scientists first examined the jacket, they merely confirmed that the blood on it belonged to the then missing Shirley Duguay. Now that they had a full murder investigation on their hands, the police sent the vital jacket back to the lab for more tests.

The new tests showed up the presence of white cat hairs which detectives realized could be very important because a large white tomcat called Snowball had been living at the same house as Beamish at the time of the murder.

If they could prove those white hairs came from that particular cat they would have a much stronger case against Beamish.

However police scientists told detectives that they would not be able to provide the evidence they needed. One detective refused to give up and used the Internet to look into the subject of DNA profiles.

While on the Net, the detective came across the work of pioneering scientist Stephen O'Brien, chief of the Cancer Research Laboratory in Frederick, Maryland, USA.

Stephen O'Brien told me, "The detective came across my name on the Internet and saw that I had been researching cat genetics and DNA for nearly twenty years. He called me up and explained the background of the case. It was in an area of Canada with very few murders and they were absolutely determined to solve this one."

O'Brien told the detective to have a professional vet take a blood sample from Snowball and send it to his lab together with the animal hairs found on the bloodstained jacket. Obviously both had to be carefully sealed to avoid cross-contamination.

"It took a lot of work," says O'Brien, "But eventually we were able to produce DNA profiles for both and they were an exact match – proving that the hairs on the jacket had come from Snowball."

To prepare for the coming court case, O'Brien and his lab had to set up a database for the DNA profiles of others cats living in the same area. They needed to prove that Snowball was the only perfect match for the incriminating hairs. This involved police officers rounding up fifty local cats so that blood samples could be taken from them as well.

When the murder trial of Douglas Beamish got under way, Stephen O'Brien was called as an expert witness. The defense lawyer acting for Beamish tried to discredit the DNA evidence, but, says O'Brien, "the science was too solid. He tried, but he couldn't do it."

Beamish was found guilty of murder and was sentenced to life imprisonment with no possibility of parole.

The Snowball case was the first time that animal or pet DNA had ever been used in a court of law to obtain a murder conviction and opened new possibilities for detectives investigating similar cases.

Since then Stephen O'Brien and his laboratory have received more than a dozen similar requests for help and he says he expects to see a growing use of the technique in many other criminal investigations.

TRAPPED BY DNA

DNA evidence was also used in the UK to bring to justice four men accused of the cruel "sport" of badger-baiting. RSPCA Inspectors had no solid evidence linking the four men to the disturbed badger sett and the dead animals until they noticed bloodstains on the men's clothes.

Although skeptical at first, the RSPCA had the stains analysed and a DNA profile extracted. It was found to match the samples taken from the dead badger, and the four men from Derbyshire were convicted.

After the trial, RSPCA Inspector Darryl Street admitted "We had no confessions and nothing to tie them down. Without the DNA evidence there would not have been a case."

Wildlife conservationists expect the technique will be used in other similar cases in the future.

DNA profiles are also playing a part in protecting rare birds and their nests.

Protected species such as the golden eagle and the peregrine falcon are often the target of thieves who steal the birds and their young to sell on the black market for as much as $1600 per animal.

The new techniques in DNA-profiling mean that scientists can now generate a profile of a bird from just one of its feathers. In the future, a feather found at a thief's home could be enough to link that person to a particular bird stolen from a particular nest, allowing criminal charges to be brought.

TERRORIST BOMBING

DNA was used as part of the evidence against the terrorist who bombed the World Trade Center in New York during 1993.

When the bomber sent a letter to the media claiming responsibility for the destruction caused, the FBI were able to extract a DNA profile from the saliva left after the envelope had been licked and sealed. When a suspect was traced and arrested through other means, his DNA profile was found to match the one from the letter.

Today an individual who sends a threatening letter or blackmail note risks being traced more than ever before, either through DNA in the saliva used to seal the letter (or lick the stamp) or through traces of DNA put there by handling the letter itself.

THE FUTURE OF DNA

DNA-profiling is sure to be used more and more in the future, but other startling developments may be around the corner as well.

Researchers are already working on ways to create a physical description of the suspect from just a sample of DNA found at a crime scene. At the moment the cutting-edge research is concentrating on isolating the DNA that is responsible for certain facial features (such as a long chin or large nose).

Creating a facial impression of a suspect from a sample of DNA is a controversial idea and many scientists think it will never happen. Others, such as forensic scientist and author Larry Ragle, are more optimistic.

Ragle predicts that in twenty to thirty years' time, police will have the technology to use a DNA sample to "generate something akin to today's composite drawings of a suspect's face."

Geneticist Stephen O'Brien agrees that such technology could be possible, but describes it as "a long way off."

Police can now obtain an individual genetic fingerprint from just a spot of blood or tiny piece of skin found at a crime scene. This DNA profile alone is enough to tell which suspects are innocent and which are guilty.

The value of DNA-profiling as a tool for solving crime cannot be overestimated.

Chapter VII

The dead can talk, Part One: dead bodies

When a body is discovered in suspicious or violent circumstances, a post-mortem is always carried out to find the cause of death. A post-mortem (usually called an autopsy in America) is a vital part of any murder investigation.

Often there may seem to be an obvious cause of death, but a proper and detailed post-mortem is still essential to confirm this and add other information.

People have been performing autopsies for nearly two thousand years. Ancient records show that several Greek doctors used the procedure to add to their medical knowledge.

After Roman Emperor Julius Caesar was assassinated, the autopsy showed that out of the twenty-three stab wounds, only one had been responsible for his death – the blow that pierced his heart.

BODY-SNATCHING

It was not until much later in the eighteenth and nineteenth centuries that the teaching of anatomy was recognized as an important branch of medical science. Post-mortems and dissections quickly became common in universities and medical

schools all over Europe.

One very unfortunate result of this new demand for corpses was the booming trade of body-snatching. In 1812 in Britain, a fresh body would fetch up to seven pounds – about six months' pay for an average worker.

The most famous pair of body snatchers, Burke and Hare, didn't bother with spades and shovels. They created their own bodies by murdering people and then selling them to the local medical school.

The Scottish pair committed sixteen murders before they were caught. Burke was executed for his crimes. His body was taken to the same medical school where he had sold his victims, and was itself dissected.

As well as making certain of the cause of death, a post-mortem also checks for poisons and toxins in the body and may also bring to light other information of use to police. On many occasions post-mortem results give the police a jumping-off point to begin their investigation.

THE TACOS MEAL MURDER

In his book *Crime Scene*, forensic scientist Larry Ragle describes an fascinating case where the autopsy results gave detectives a rather unexpected clue to help start their enquiries.

A woman's body had been found just outside the town of Oceanside in California. She had been murdered by a blow to the head and police had few clues and no suspects. The woman's family told detectives she had been hitchhiking back from a job interview when she was killed.

A post-mortem always includes an analysis of the contents of the victim's stomach. In this case they revealed that the woman's last meal had been Mexican tacos which had been eaten no more than thirty minutes before her death.

Police began to make enquiries at every restaurant that sold tacos within half an hour's drive of where the woman's body had been found. They soon got lucky.

After only a few restaurants, detectives found a waitress who remembered the victim buying her food and then walking to the bar across the street. In the bar, officers were told that the woman had been seen leaving with a regular customer – a Marine whom the barman knew by name.

Detectives visited the man and during a search of his car found the victim's purse. Later that same evening, the man admitted the murder and was charged.

The results of the autopsy had given detectives information that had saved many hours of police work and, thanks to the victim's last meal, the killer had been caught within twenty-four hours.

COLLECTING EVIDENCE

The purpose of a post-mortem is for the medical examiner to come to a definite conclusion as to exactly how someone died. No possible cause of death, likely or unlikely, natural or unnatural, should be left uninvestigated.

If the body has not yet been identified – either because no identification was found or more likely in a murder case because it has been deliberately removed – then identifying the deceased will be a priority.

As we saw with the Luton sack murder in chapter one, some murderers go to great lengths to try to hide the identity of their victim, believing that it will make the crime unsolvable. However, few victims remain unidentified for long, especially with the recent advances made in DNA-profiling.

When a post-mortem is performed neither the medical examiner nor detectives know where the enquiry will head in the future. A case that begins looking like a clear-cut suicide may develop after forensic work into a murder enquiry – or even vice versa.

A piece of evidence that may seem irrelevant now could turn out to be vital later when the case comes to court. Evidence collected first-hand from the body can be the only objective testimony detectives have to work with.

THE TIME OF DEATH

One of the most important findings of the post-mortem for detectives is the time of death. Until recently, this was estimated based on rigor mortis – the tightening of muscles that occurs after death. It is from the phenomenon of rigor mortis that American police officers originally got the term "stiff" for a dead body.

Examiners today have a more accurate method. Using a thin needle, a sample of vitreous humor – a jelly-like substance found inside the eyeball – is taken. After death occurs, red blood cells in the vitreous humor break down at a reliable and predictable rate which gives the examiner a better system for determining the time of death.

THE POST-MORTEM

During the post-mortem, photographs and videotape are used to provide a record of injuries and other visual evidence. The medical examiner speaks into a tape recorder, describing his findings as he goes along. These verbal notes are later transcribed and provide the bulk of the examiner's final report.

When the post-mortem begins, the body will still be wrapped in the plastic sheet that it was placed in at the crime scene. This is carefully removed and any loose trace evidence (such as gravel or earth) is collected and labeled.

The first stage is the careful and systematic removal of the deceased's clothes. Each item is carefully studied for any hairs, fibers, or blood stains that may be present.

The fingernails are closely examined for any materials that may be trapped under them. Particularly if there has been a struggle or fight, traces of the attacker's skin tissue or fibers from his or her clothes might be present.

Next begins the external examination of the body. In many cases such as a shooting or stabbing, the injury can be very obvious. In all instances, the entry angle of the wound and its depth are noted. A slight difference in angle may prove or disprove an individual's self-defense argument later in court.

After the clothes have been removed, the entire surface of the body, both front and back, is examined and samples of the deceased's hair are taken and stored.

By examining the hands it is possible to tell if any gunshot residue is present – vital evidence in proving that the subject had fired a weapon shortly before his or her own death.

DISSECTING THE BODY

The next stage is the dissection of the body, and this begins with the examiner making an incision down the middle of the body, starting at the bottom of the neck.

Blood samples are taken to be tested for alcohol content, and may also be analyzed for poison and other toxins. If appropriate, a DNA profile can be produced from the blood sample.

The stomach is removed and cut open over a large bowl. The contents are recorded and – as we saw in the tacos meal murder case – can provide useful information about the deceased's last movements.

Other internal organs are also examined, the most important being the heart, lungs, kidneys, and liver.

The lungs can be examined for traces of toxic gases and also for dust and other airborne trace evidence that may be helpful.

If death was caused by drowning, the lungs will usually contain water with algae in it. This can be matched back to the river or sea where the body was found to discount the possibility that the victim was drowned elsewhere (for example, in a bath of tap water) and dumped at sea afterwards.

The presence of diatoms (tiny water-dwelling organisms) throughout the body can be taken to mean that the person was alive when he or she went into the water. The absence of diatoms apart from a few in the lungs means that the body was already dead when it hit the water.

After the examination is over the body is sown back up. If the deceased is the subject of a criminal investigation then the body will be preserved in a refrigerated storage unit, in case further tests are needed in the future.

THE POISONER'S GAMBIT

Perhaps the murderer's best hope of getting away with his or her crime is making the killing look like a natural death so a post-mortem is not carried out. However, even buried, a victim can still rise up again to cast the bony finger of accusation at the killer.

For a long period in England, poison was the murderer's favorite option, giving rise to many famous cases involving arsenic, cyanide, and strychnine. Most poisons are quite easily detected, but only if searched for by a suspicious medical examiner.

On May 24, 1934, Arthur Major died after two days of terrible illness, his death being blamed on a tin of bad corned beef. A death certificate was issued and his funeral was arranged with most of the local village invited to pay their last respects.

Everything would have proceeded according to plan, except that the day before the funeral the police received a strange anonymous letter. It claimed that a dog belonging to one of the Majors' neighbors had suddenly dropped dead after eating food scraps put out by Ethel Major, Arthur's wife.

The dog's body was quickly dug up and examined. A large dose of the poison strychnine was detected, and police officers just managed to interrupt Arthur Major's funeral in time. They took his body away for a post-mortem and discovered that the "bad" corned beef was only bad because it had been laced with strychnine.

A dose of strychnine as small as 100 milligrams is fatal and victims suffer horrific spasms, dying with their face muscles fixed in a larger-than-life grin called "risus sardonicus."

Before police had a chance to tell Ethel Major of their post-mortem findings she informed them, "I am shocked. I had no idea that my husband had died of strychnine poisoning"

– an unfortunate and rather careless thing to say as no one else had mentioned strychnine at all.

If Ethel had not fed the scraps of corned beef to her neighbor's dog, she would almost certainly have got away with her husband's murder. Instead, she was found guilty and hanged in Hull Prison.

THE ROTTING CORPSE

Often a body does not reach the post-mortem table straight after death and the process of decomposition may have already started or be well advanced.

Strictly speaking, decomposition will begin as soon as life has ceased, but in practical terms it takes weeks, if not months, for a corpse to begin to disintegrate. A body left out in the air will decompose much more quickly than one floating in water or buried underground.

It takes about a year in the open air to reduce a body to a skeleton, leaving investigators with just bare bones to work from. Although a much more difficult task, forensic scientists have proved more than equal to the challenge on many occasions.

In 1989, workmen digging a trench in a suburban garden in Cardiff, Wales found a skeleton – all that remained of a human body. Experts estimated they had been there for more than a decade.

NAMING THE DEAD

A facial reconstruction based on the shape of the skull was created and pictures of the resulting clay bust were circulated to the media. Within two days, a social worker had given the skeleton a name. She was Karen Welsh, who had disappeared ten years before in the Cardiff area.

A broadcast on the BBC's *Crimewatch* program also resulted in one of the girl's murderer's being identified, but to ensure a conviction in a court of law police would have to prove the identity of the bones beyond reasonable doubt.

Detectives asked Oxford biochemist Erika Hagelberg to produce a DNA profile of the skeleton that could then be matched with members of Karen Welsh's family who were still alive.

Erika began the complex task by sandblasting the bones clean then grinding the residue into a powder. This process gave her plenty of DNA to work with, but she discovered that 99 percent of it was non-human and belonged to a fungus that had contaminated the bones during their long period outdoors.

With so little human DNA to work from, a new technique was needed to obtain a reliable profile and Erika combined her talents with those of Dr. Alec Jeffreys – the father of DNA-profiling. Together they perfected a method of reading much smaller samples of DNA and created the profile that the detectives needed. It was a match with the Welsh family and the skeleton had been given an official identity.

It was the first time that DNA evidence from decayed bones had been used in a court case and two men on trial ended up being convicted of a crime they had carried out more than ten years before.

THE ACID BATH MURDERS

A post-mortem can tell detectives a lot about how the subject died, what sort of person he or she was when alive, and what were his or her final actions before death. Although the corpse cannot speak, many murderers have been caught out by the silent evidence given by their victims.

Apart from making a murder look like death by natural causes, perhaps a killer's best plan is to make sure that no one ever finds the body. An English killer called John Haigh tried to do exactly that using a large drum of corrosive sulphuric acid to dissolve his victims.

Police investigating the disappearance of Mrs. Durand-Deacon visited a small factory owned by Haigh in Crawley, Sussex. Mrs. Durand-Deacon, a wealthy widow, had last been seen in the company of Haigh, and police were already suspicious. Inside the factory, they found the drum of deadly acid and a .38 Webley revolver that had recently been fired.

John Haigh remained supremely confident that the police would not be able to prove foul play, boasting, "You can't prove murder without a body. Mrs. Durand-Deacon no longer exists. There is not a trace of her. I have destroyed her with acid and as there is no body there can surely be no trial."

ANOTHER FINE MESS

Police dumped the contents of the drum over the floor and, getting down on their hands and knees, sifted through the gruesome sludge.

Finding something hard, a police scientist washed off the smelly grey gunge and found that he was holding Mrs.

Durand-Deacon's false teeth in his hand. They were made of plastic and had not dissolved with the rest of her. The false teeth were later identified by Mrs. Durand-Deacon's dentist.

John Haigh eventually confessed to several other murders, having disposed of the bodies by the same ingenious but flawed technique.

Speaking of Mrs. Durand-Deacon who was known for her full figure, Haigh offered the opinion that "Fat people were far more difficult to dissolve than thin and Mrs. Durand-Deacon was a confounded woman. Far more trouble than any of the others."

For all his efforts, Haigh would probably have been better off making it look like natural causes. One of England's most famous murderers, he was executed at Wandsworth Prison on August 10, 1949.

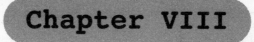

Chapter VIII

The dead can talk,
Part Two: strange tales

A killer may think that doing away with his or her victim will be the end of his or her troubles. Sometimes, however, the dead just won't stay dead.

A ghost returning from the grave to haunt his or her murderer has been a popular theme in plays and books for centuries, but such events are not just limited to fiction.

A VERY HELPFUL GHOST

A very cooperative ghost proved to be the answer to one of investigator Allan Pinkerton's cases in September 1895.

Pinkerton had been assigned to investigate the murder of a bank clerk and the theft of $130,000, equivalent to about five million dollars at today's prices.

Within the first few days of his investigation, Pinkerton became certain that county clerk and seemingly respectable citizen Alexander P. Drysdale was responsible. Pinkerton now had a prime suspect, but absolutely no evidence against him, so he called in three colleagues to help.

By an unlikely but happy coincidence, Mr. Green, one of Pinkerton's assistants, was an almost perfect lookalike for the murdered bank teller. A plan began to form in Pinkerton's mind. Using fake blood and white powder, Pinkerton made up his assistant to look like the ghost of the dead man.

TWILIGHT HAUNTING

Pinkerton had another assistant persuade Alexander Drysdale to go for a walk just before sunset. The assistant led Drysdale towards to Rocky Creek – a local landmark that was supposedly haunted.

Just as dusk set in, a terrible moaning sound began to echo along the darkened canyon. A few moments later, Green came stumbling along the creek floor, looking every inch the restless spirit seeking revenge.

Drysdale let out a terrified scream. His walking companion pretended to see nothing at all, which only served to increase his alarm.

Worse was to come, as Pinkerton ordered his ghost to go on a number of midnight hauntings around the unfortunate suspect's home. Drysdale watched with terror as the phantom circled his house before disappearing into the night. Unsurprisingly, he began to suffer from terrible nightmares.

The climax to Pinkerton's plan came as he placed Drysdale under arrest and took him to the bank where the robbery had taken place. As they entered the building, the ghost staggered up from where he had been murdered, dripping with blood. Drysdale fainted on the spot.

When he regained consciousness, Drysdale needed only the slightest amount of encouragement to make a full confession.

A VOICE FROM THE GRAVE

While Pinkerton's ghost was a convenient fake, the strange case of nurse Teresita Basa's murder is enough to send shivers down any spine. During a police investigation, the voice of a murdered woman seemed actually to speak from beyond the grave to name the man who killed her.

On the evening of February 21, 1977 Teresita Basa, a forty-eight-year-old nurse who worked at Chicago's Edgewater Hospital, was murdered in her apartment.

There was no sign of forced entry, so detectives reasoned that she must have known her killer and let him or her inside. After the attack, her killer searched the apartment and stole family jewelry. Before he or she left, the attacker set the apartment on fire in an attempt to destroy as much evidence as possible.

Officers questioned Teresita's family and friends, but none

of them could suggest a reason for the murder and all of them had alibis for the night in question. The next few weeks brought the police no new leads and detectives became resigned to the case remaining unsolved. Until, that is, they heard about the startling dreams of Remy Chua.

Remy (short for Remibias) Chua worked as a nurse in the same hospital as Teresita Basa and like Teresita was a Filipina.

About two weeks after Teresita's murder, Remy was taking a well-earned nap in one of the staff rooms. As she woke up, she became aware of someone standing in the doorway. Remy opened her mouth to say hello, but before she could speak, she saw who the figure was – Teresita Basa. Remy was terrified and ran straight out of the room.

Before she had gone to sleep, Remy had been talking about Teresita's murder with a fellow worker. Surely Remy's "visitor" was really just a bad dream that she had remembered as she woke up?

Remy certainly preferred to think so, but even stranger events were about to take place.

THE KILLER'S FACE

A few days later Remy began to experience a series of very disturbing dreams. In the dreams, she watched the events of the night of Teresita's murder.

She saw Teresita open her apartment door and greet someone she knew. But however hard she tried, Remy could not make out the man's face. Next, in her dream she saw the attack and the theft of the jewelry.

Remy had the same dream for three nights running and on the third night she saw the face of the killer for the first time. It was a man that she recognized. A man who worked at the hospital.

The events of the next night were even more frightening. Seeing that she was having another nightmare, Remy's husband Joseph decided to wake her up. He was about to shake her when she suddenly opened her eyes.

Shivers ran along Joseph's spine, as his wife began to speak in a completely different voice from her usual one.

The voice claimed to be Teresita Basa and told the terrified Joseph that she wanted him to tell the police who had murdered her. Eventually, Joseph coaxed the killer's identity from the voice – Allan Showery.

The voice told Joseph how Showery agreed to repair her television set, but when she had let him inside her apartment, he suddenly attacked her. The voice also dictated a telephone number saying that it belonged to her family and that they would be able to identify the missing jewelry when it was found.

ENTER THE POLICE

Joseph and Remy knew that they had to go to the police. They visited a police station and told detectives the whole story. Both knew there was little chance of them being taken seriously, but they felt they had to at least try.

Detectives noted the details, but seemed unimpressed with their ghost story.

It was months before detectives visited Remy and her husband to check their story about the dreams. Having no other leads to follow, reluctant officers finally decided to visit Allan Showery and question him.

Showery had been questioned once before, simply because he knew Teresita, but that interview had found nothing suspicious.

The first hint that detectives might be on the right track came when Allan Showery's girlfriend changed her story removing his alibi. When Showery himself made an entrance, both detectives noticed that he now seemed nervous.

Acting on a hunch, one of the detectives told Showery that as a matter of routine they would have to take his finger-prints. Showery bolted for the door, but was tackled and wrestled to the ground before he could escape.

A search of his apartment found Teresita's missing jewelry. He confessed in police custody and was charged with murder.

When police phoned the telephone number that had been dictated in the dead of night by Teresita's voice, detectives found themselves talking to one of Teresita's cousins. The cousin gladly agreed to travel into town to identify the stolen jewelry.

GOING TO TRIAL

Such an unusual case of course had an unusual ending. It went to court not once, but twice.

Before the first trial, Showery withdrew his confession and so the police case depended largely on the testimony of Teresita's ghost.

Newspapers ran headlines like the *Chicago Tribune*'s "DID VOICE FROM THE GRAVE NAME KILLER?" – none of which helped the prosecution's case.

Showery's lawyer, Daniel E. Radakovich, tried to have the

entire case thrown out of court on the grounds that a voice from beyond the grave was not justifiable cause for arrest or for a search of the apartment. Judge Frank Barbaro disagreed however, and the trial went ahead.

The jury were unable to reach a verdict. Some jurors were open to the possibility of spirits and psychic communication, while others just laughed at the idea. A mistrial was declared and the case had to be tried again.

Detectives feared that Showery would escape punishment at the second trial, but suddenly, and against the advice of his lawyers, he changed his plea to guilty.

No one could work out why. Did his conscience finally get the better of him? Or perhaps he woke up one night to find that he had an unexpected visitor in his cell. Either way, Showery was convicted of murder and went to prison.

THE WOMAN WHO KNEW TOO MUCH

Some psychics have been known to get themselves into a great deal of trouble thanks to their seemingly impossible knowledge of certain crimes.

Etta Louise Smith was not the first person to discover that a little psychic knowledge can be a dangerous thing.

Her first and only psychic experience resulted in her arrest for murder and five days spent in jail. Etta Louise Smith had never thought of herself as psychic until one peculiar day in December 1980.

Etta, a 39-year-old single mother with two children, lived in Los Angeles, California. She worked for an aircraft company and one lunchtime she found herself discussing the city's crime rate with a fellow worker.

Both women were worried about the rising tide of crime and the conversation turned to the recent disappearance of a woman called Melanie Uribe. Melanie had vanished a few days before – just one more missing person among the thousands reported every year.

PSYCHIC VISIONS

Later that same week, Etta Smith was watching television at home when she had her first and only psychic experience.

A weird feeling of warmth and well-being swept over her and in the middle of this, Etta somehow knew that Melanie Uribe had been murdered. Etta also knew that her undiscovered body was lying in one of the windswept desert canyons on the edge of the city.

In a television interview afterwards, Etta described what had happened. "It was as if I had suddenly heard a voice say 'she's not in a house.' Then I saw where her body was as clearly as if it were a photograph in front of me. It was like a picture of a canyon road on the edge of town. I didn't know the canyon's name, but I knew exactly where it was located."

Etta even saw what clothes Melanie had been wearing when she had been killed. She didn't have a clue where this information was coming from, but she made sure that she memorized the exact spot that she had been shown.

As soon as the vision ended, Etta drove straight to her local police station, the Foothill Division. She was soon joined by Detective Lee Ryan who was in charge of investigating Melanie's disappearance. Etta told him everything that she had "seen."

When the detective produced a map of the area she even picked out the exact place – it was called Lopez Canyon.

The detective thanked Etta for her interest and she went home, unsure if the police were going to search the canyon.

FINDING THE BODY

It was difficult for Etta to get the case out of her mind. Her thoughts kept returning to her strange vision. She was more certain than ever that she was right about the location of the body.

The next day she told her two children about both her vision and her trip to the police station. They were excited and impressed that their own mother had the psychic clues to solve a murder case.

They insisted that she take them out to the canyon itself. At first, Etta resisted, but eventually her own curiosity got the better of her. She was still unsure if the police were going to search the canyon, and decided she might as well take a look herself.

The family climbed into Etta's car and drove out of town towards the desolate canyon, high in the hills above Los Angeles.

They all began to look around, with Etta's two children running ahead of her to cover more ground. Etta herself was both excited and afraid. Then Etta's daughter, Tina, caught sight of something white lying among the dusty rocks of the canyon. There, exactly as Etta had seen in her vision, was the body of Melanie Uribe.

The now frightened family rushed back to their car and raced out of the canyon. On the way back to town, they saw a police patrol and flagged it down.

CHARGED WITH MURDER

It was then Etta Smith's troubles really began. Now that the police had a murder case on their hands, Etta found that they also had a prime suspect – her. As far as the police were concerned Etta knew too much about the murder not to be involved.

How else could she know the exact whereabouts of the victim and even what she had been wearing?

Etta had only been trying to help the police, but now she found herself facing a murder charge! She was held in police custody and questioned for five days.

Only one man, Detective Lee Ryan, the man she had initially spoken to, believed she was telling the truth. He could not explain how she knew what she did, but he did believe she was completely innocent.

THE REAL KILLERS

Etta Smith might well have stood trial for the murder except for one lucky break.

In another part of the city, a routine police patrol stopped a car for a minor motoring offense. When the car's registration number was checked it was found that the current driver, an 18-year-old student, did not actually own the car. He was taken into custody for questioning.

The student, Kenneth Newman, did not know he was being arrested for the motor offense and believed that the police had other more serious reasons. Almost immediately, Newman confessed, not to car theft, but to murder.

The car he had been driving belonged to Melanie Uribe. He and two fellow students, Andrew Keel and John Holland, had murdered the nurse and dumped her body in the desert canyon believing that she would never be found. They had then taken her car and driven back to town in it.

The three students went to trial and were sentenced to thirty years each for the crime.

Etta was released by the police, but she found the whole experience a difficult and disturbing one. She decided to sue them for wrongful arrest, and hired lawyer James Blatt to represent her.

The case took over six years to come to court, but in March 1987 eventually Etta received over $25,000 in damages for false arrest.

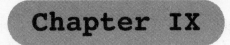

Chapter IX

The sleeping psychic

Psychics often find themselves being consulted by police officers as a last resort during a particularly difficult case. There is, however, one psychic who has been correct so often that he is under orders from the police to fax them his predictions every single day.

To those familiar with his strange talents, Chris Robinson is known as the dream detective. The 46-year-old psychic lives in Bedfordshire, England and claims to literally dream the future.

Every night while Chris sleeps, he keeps a blank pad of paper and a pen by his bedside. While he is asleep and dreaming, he scribbles down notes, unconsciously writing down what he is seeing and what is happening in the dreams.

Sometimes, if the dream was vivid, Chris will be able to remember it when he wakes up. On other occasions he has only the notes in his dream diary to go on. The dreams that Chris has can be very complex and usually need what he calls "decoding" by him the next day.

TECHNICALLY DEAD

When I met Chris, he told me that like many other psychics he had had a close brush with death much earlier in his life.

"When I was nine years old, I had open-heart surgery at Guy's Hospital in London. Following that, when I was sixteen, I had a terrible motorcycle accident. I had very bad head injuries and was rushed to hospital. For a short time, my heart actually stopped beating and, for a few seconds, I was technically dead."

Chris's strange dreams began in 1989 when he was staying overnight with a friend. He had a dream in which his grandmother, who had died years before, appeared. The dream happened in the middle of the night and she told Chris that his car was being stolen at that very moment.

"Next day when I got back to my own house a neighbour came out and told me that her husband had got up in the night to chase off some thieves who were trying to break into my car. It turned out that he had stayed up most of the night guarding it."

At the time Chris put it down to coincidence, but stranger incidents were to follow. Chris began to dream about a deceased soldier called Robert who kept returning night after night.

The soldier told Chris there would be a fire on a particular ferry heading across the North Sea towards Sweden. This was one of the first dreams Chris reported to the police. Chris was proved correct, there really was a fire and the police began to take a real interest in his dreams.

WARNINGS OF DEATH

The soldier continued to visit Chris in his dreams, and events soon took an even more serious turn. He began to deliver more warnings, this time about terrorists and bombs on mainland Britain. In his dream, the soldier took Chris to a hotel in Cheltenham and showed him five terrorists preparing for a bomb campaign.

"I gave all the information I had to the police as soon as I woke up. It was only later that I discovered that the hotel I had dreamed about was already under surveillance for suspected terrorist activity."

After many more dreams in which Chris accurately predicted where and when bombs would explode, he was contacted by a man from MI5 who asked for all the dream material to be sent to him. Now that people in power were taking him seriously, Chris hoped he could use his dreams to help save lives.

BOMB ATTACK

In November 1991, Chris began to dream about a terrorist attack on the town of St. Albans in Bedfordshire near where he lives. The dreams contained the postcode for St. Albans as well as the tell-tale sign of wild vicious dogs which always meant terrorists.

Chris saw the two terrorists walk down the high street in St. Albans carrying a bomb in a large envelope. Just as they pushed it through the letterbox of a bank, it exploded, killing them both and destroying the bank.

For several nights running, Chris dreamt of bombs in St. Albans, usually a sign that the attack would happen very soon. Chris got in touch with his police contacts.

"By now they were listening to what I had to say. What I did not know was that an army band was due to play in the public hall near the bank on the night I predicted the attack would happen. The police took my warning seriously and that night they had extra surveillance keeping watch on the area."

SAVING LIVES

Two of the surveillance officers on the roof of a main-street store saw a suspicious-looking pair of people walking towards the bank and reported it. The concert was about to end, but rather than take a chance, the band was told to keep playing and the crowd was kept inside. It was just as well.

As the pair of terrorists put the bomb through the letter-box of the bank, it exploded – killing them both exactly as it had happened in Chris's dream. If the crowd had been coming out of the hall at that moment, many of them would have died as well.

DRUG-RUNNING

Chris Robinson has been of help to police not just with terrorist attacks – he has also helped to put drug smugglers out of business.

In one dream he found himself on an Air India plane about to land at London's Heathrow airport. As Chris got off the plane he heard someone in the dream mention the number of the flight and the fact that it was a Thursday.

Chris found himself waiting to reclaim his suitcase at the baggage carousel. He waited until the other passengers had all collected their cases, and there was just one dark leather case left. That had to be his.

As Chris walked through Customs holding the case, he was called over and asked to open it. The Customs Officer took just a few seconds to sort through the layer of loosely packed clothes on top and reveal what was hidden below . . . illegal drugs.

When Chris woke the next morning, he immediately checked his dream notes. "I wanted to make sure I'd written down the flight number and the day. They were there, but that wasn't all. I'd drawn a sketch of the suitcase as well."

Chris already had contacts in HM Customs and Excise and he got in touch with them. They already knew of Chris's dreams and took him seriously enough to arrange for him to come to Heathrow airport.

On Thursday Chris found out that there was a plane coming in from India that had the same flight number. A wave of excitement passed through the Customs officers waiting with him.

ON THE SMUGGLER'S TRAIL

After the aircraft had landed, Chris and the Customs men sorted through nearly 1,000 suitcases looking for the one that Chris had sketched. Finally they managed to narrow the possibilities down to just nine and it was up to Chris to make the final choice.

Chris made the final decision on pure instinct and the Customs men used a skeleton key to pick the lock and open the case. Taking out the contents, they found that the suitcase had a false bottom. Below that were several plastic bags stuffed with illegal drugs.

Chris had hit the jackpot and the Customs men were delighted.

For Chris it was one of his most rewarding nights of sleep so far. "It was like an instant result. I had the dream, which was one of my clearest ever, and it turned out to be spot-on."

A BUSMAN'S HOLIDAY

Chris told me about another incident that happened on the way back from a holiday on the island of Cyprus. On the night before his flight back to England, Chris had a very short dream in which he saw three soldiers being arrested for smuggling drugs into Britain.

The three soldiers had featured in a very small section of that night's dreams and Chris thought no more about it, until he was waiting to board his plane at the airport.

In the departure lounge, Chris noticed three men in their twenties with short army-style haircuts. He watched as another man approached them and secretively swapped bags with one of the young men. This immediately aroused Chris's suspicions, and during the flight Chris asked the pilot to radio ahead to Customs control at Luton airport.

When the three men tried to go straight through the "Nothing to Declare" channel they were pulled over by a Customs officer and their bags were searched. Hidden in the third holdall, under a bundle of dirty shirts, was a large package containing drugs.

NEW PREMONITIONS

Nearly ten years after the strange dreams began, Chris continues to dream night after night. Every dream brings new predictions and premonitions of the future. Chris himself cannot explain how his powers work, but over the years he has become convinced that the information is coming from the spirit world – wherever people go when they die.

"In one way I can't wait to get there and find out for myself," Chris told me. "But than again I've got a family and young kids, so I don't think I'm in any hurry just yet."

Chris told me that his strongest and most accurate dreams are always those where he believes he is being contacted by the spirit of a person who is now dead. "Sometimes it might be a deceased police officer, or my grandmother, or a friend. The dreams with people in them are always the clearest, and usually turn out to be the most accurate."

HITS AND MISSES

Chris is the first to admit that he is not always right. Often his dreams are too vague to pinpoint any specific event before it happens and can only really be understood afterwards.

Over the years, though, Chris has managed to get better at decoding what the dreams mean.

"When words are repeated in the dream diary in capital letters it is a sign that I am being given the postcode of a location. If I see dogs in a dream, that means terrorist activity and if there are meat pies lying around I know it means that people are going to be killed."

The timing and frequency of the dreams is also important. "I hardly ever make a prediction based on just one dream. I have to dream variations of the same thing three nights running before I can be really confident about it. Most of the things I dream come true within three weeks."

A UNIQUE CASE

Even for a psychic, Chris Robertson is very unusual. Most psychics receive their information while they are awake – even if they are in a trance or otherworld state. Chris's predictions are always made in his sleep.

Chris is also unusual because the authorities that he works with – the police, the security services, Customs and Excise – are willing to go on the record to back up Chris's extraordinary stories.

Alex Hall, an Ex-Detective Chief Inspector formerly with the Regional Crime Squad worked with Chris for five years. Alex told me, "Chris was getting in touch with police forces all over the country and so I was asked to be his official contact. My job was to act as a filter for the information he was producing."

With over thirty years' experience in the police force, Alex had an open-minded but skeptical attitude to Chris's dreams. "I think he found me difficult to work with because I would always look for other ways that he could have got the information." However, Alex admits, "on many occasions when the dreams turned out to be true, I could find no other explanation to account for what Chris had told me."

Chris is probably the most documented psychic in the world. Every day he sends a fax of the previous night's dreams to the police or MI5 depending on whom he is working with at the time.

Chris believes that many people are more psychic than they give themselves credit for. "It could be just another word for intuition. Like a policeman's intuition, where his life may depend on him listening to his instincts."

ADVENTURES ON SCREEN

Chris has appeared on numerous television programs where sometimes the producer will demand that he proves his abilities before appearing on screen.

As a test for one program on Central Television, a metal box was sealed with three objects inside and Chris was asked to dream what they were. Over the next couple of nights, Chris got strong dream images for two of the objects.

For the first one, Chris found himself in a huge stone building sawing a piece of wood out of the floor. The second one Chris found more difficult to actually name, but he knew that it had belonged to the producer's mother and had been on her dining room table, although he felt that it was now owned by the woman's granddaughter.

Chris explained his predictions at the television studio and they opened the box. The first object was revealed as a piece of wood that one of the production crew had cut out of the floor of Nottingham Castle.

The second object was a silver ring. The amazed producer explained that it was made of silver originally owned by his mother. When she had died, her set of silver cutlery had been melted down and made into jewelery for her grand-daughters.

Chris had proved exactly right with two out of the three objects.

A VERY STRANGE TALENT

To the outside world, Chris seems a down-to-earth man still struggling to come to terms with the unexpected turn his life took when he started to have his extraordinary dreams in 1989. Despite the numerous problems caused by the dreams, Chris feels that they have enriched his life by show-ing him things he would otherwise never have seen.

Paranormal expert Lorne Mason says: "Of all the psychics in the world who work with police departments, Chris Robinson is a special case. I don't think anyone has scored more hits than him or has ever been so well documented. No one can explain Chris's dreams. All you can say is that they do seem to keep coming true."

Chris told me he has two main ambitions for the future. The first is to be able to prove that his abilities really do exist to more and more people. The second, and much more important, ambition is to continue to help the police and security services save lives whenever he can.

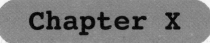

Chapter X

Computers and crime

Computers offer unparalleled opportunities for business-men, teachers, and students. Unfortunately, they also offer new opportunities to criminals. It is now possible to rob a bank in virtual reality.

Today, a clever computer crook can steal millions of dollars

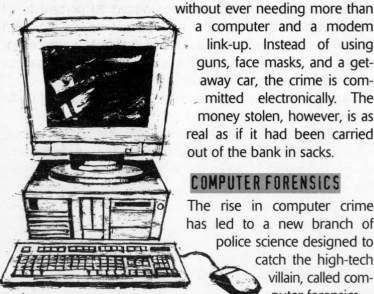

without ever needing more than a computer and a modem link-up. Instead of using guns, face masks, and a get-away car, the crime is committed electronically. The money stolen, however, is as real as if it had been carried out of the bank in sacks.

COMPUTER FORENSICS

The rise in computer crime has led to a new branch of police science designed to catch the high-tech villain, called computer forensics.

Unlike a normal thief, computer criminals leave no fingerprints or other physical evidence. To catch them and to gather evidence that can be used in court, the police need experts as skilled in computer wizardry as the criminals themselves.

London's Scotland Yard set up its own Computer Crime Unit in the 1980s and since then many independent firms have been formed to offer freelance specialists in the field.

Most computer crime and fraud is committed by people within the organization being robbed. It is comparatively easy for an employee of a bank to create a false account and have money regularly paid into it from other accounts.

THE NEW YORK BANK SCAM

A computer operator working in a New York bank decided to use an ingenious scheme to net herself money. She altered the computer program that added bank charges onto customers' accounts. Her alteration added 10 percent to all the service charges with the actual amounts varying from twenty cents to several dollars. She then opened an account under the fake name of Miss Harriet Plimpton and had all the extra money diverted into it.

Although each amount was small, together it added up to be nearly $1,000 per month.

It took over two years (by which time the employee had taken home $25,000) for her scam to be noticed – and even then it was spotted by luck. In all that time not one customer had noticed the extra bank charges he or she was paying.

The woman was eventually caught when a different department in the bank tried to send information to Miss Plimpton and found that there was no record of her address or other paperwork on file. Following an investigation into this suspicious state of affairs, the real culprit was quickly identified.

KEYBOARD ROBBERY

This case illustrates one of the biggest problems of computer crime. Computers are good at handling huge amounts of data or money – but only when programmed properly. Unlike a human worker, a computer will not object or become suspicious when told to do something dishonest – as in the New York bank scam.

When an irregularity is discovered, tracing the electronic paper-trail can prove next to impossible. Even if police do find the culprit, the company is often very reluctant to press charges. Why? Because big companies live in fear of bad publicity that can affect their profits or share price.

There is nothing more embarrassing for a company than having to admit that its own employees have been successfully stealing hundreds of thousands of dollars over a long period of time. As a result, computer crimes in the world of big business are often hushed up and never reach a court of law.

Experts estimate that world-wide computer crime is rising and it is one of the hardest forms of criminal activity to crack down on. Often a case will cross international boundaries – a computer in one country stealing money from a bank in another – and cooperation between many different police forces maybe needed.

BLACKMAIL BY COMPUTER VIRUS

Another type of computer criminal is the blackmailer. In the last ten years, there have been many cases of firms being held to ransom by people infecting a company's computer system with an electronic virus.

The virus may be placed in the company's computer network by an employee, or over the telephone from another location. A virus program is specially designed to copy itself into the computer's normal programs with the aim of slowing them down or destroying valuable data.

After a company's system has been deliberately infected with a computer virus, a message may appear on the system's monitor screens ordering that a large sum of cash be paid to the blackmailer. The blackmailer promises that when the money is delivered, he or she will provide the company with a special code that will kill the virus when it is entered into the system.

A business that falls victim to this kind of blackmail plot must decide on the best course of action: whether to pay the money demanded, or whether to call the police and try to catch the blackmailers.

It can be a difficult decision because once a sophisticated virus gets into a computer system, it is very hard to isolate or fight against it without the proper codes to shut it down. Most experts agree that where a virus is concerned, prevention is better (and a lot cheaper) than cure.

THE BLACK BARON

In November 1995 British police convicted 26-year-old Christopher Pile as the brains behind a particularly nasty breed of computer virus.

Pile was known as the Black Baron in computer circles and he was eventually sent to prison for eighteen months thanks to the technical help of computer forensics expert Jim Bates. Bates runs the freelance firm of Computer Forensics based in Leicestershire and he is asked for assistance by police forces from all over the country.

When police first arrested Pile it looked as if he had wiped all potential evidence against him off his various computer systems. However, Bates had special software tools that allowed him to search through more then forty computer discs of material to find the only virus-writing program that remained.

COMPUTER COPS

Although computer technology has its unlawful uses, it is also of great help to police forces all over the world.

Computers are regularly used by police to check finger-prints found at a crime scene with those of known offenders whose prints are already on record. In the past this time-con-suming procedure was done by officers working by hand and it could literally take months.

Today there are computer databases of hundreds of thou-sands of fingerprints and DNA profiles that can be computer-checked in mere hours.

During any large police enquiry detectives often find themselves swamped underneath a mountain of paperwork and eyewitness reports. To assist British police involved in major investigations, the Home Office set up a computer sys-tem called HOLMES in 1987.

HOLMES AT WORK

Named after Sir Arthur Conan Doyle's fictional detective, HOLMES (standing for Home Office Large Major Enquiry System) allows detectives to enter all information about a cer-tain case so that the machine can collate all the data and allow police to access it easily.

For example, a detective could request data on blue vans and HOLMES would provide details of any and all eyewit-ness reports or interviews that mentioned such a car. Since its introduction, HOLMES has been superseded by faster systems, but the method behind them remains the same.

In America, the FBI have a very similar computer system called "Big Floyd" which is used in major cases to the same effect. Other facilities such as the National Crime Information Centre (NCIC) let different police forces across the United States pool their information to mutual benefit.

Not all computers used by the police are large multi-million-dollar systems. In many countries police officers have a small computer terminal in their patrol cars. This gives them access to the latest information on crime in their area and enables them to check the registration numbers of any suspicious cars on-line to see if they are stolen.

Officers can also check to see if an individual has a criminal record or if he or she is wanted for any other crimes.

COMPUTER TRICKS

Inside police stations computers are put to even more specialized uses. Computer-imaging is often used to clean up grainy or blurred images from surveillance cameras that have caught criminals on videotape. Often the image from a bank's cameras needs to be made larger and also digitally enhanced to get a clear picture of the suspect.

In cases where someone has been missing for a period of many years, police do not have a current photograph of that person to help with their search. Computers can come to the rescue once again with a special software package called Computer Ageing.

An old photograph of the person is scanned into the computer and the program is able to automatically age the image any number of years to show what he or she may look like today.

In 1989, an age-enhanced photograph resulted in the capture of a five-times killer after he was recognized by his

neighbors. Although it had been eighteen years since the man had disappeared, the computer ageing was so good that his new neighbors recognized him immediately.

COMPUTERS IN THE WITNESS BOX

Because computers are so widely used in everyday life – even by criminals and in organized crime – they offer a whole new avenue of investigation for police to explore.

Criminals who use computers to record and store information or simply to write letters on leave an electronic trail behind them. The users may think that they have erased all the incriminating files on their machine with a simple "DELETE" command. However this is usually far from the truth.

A "DELETE" command does not destroy the information in question – it just stops the computer saving it in a specially-named file. Often the contents of a "deleted" file will be floating around the hard disk for weeks after the owner thinks they have been dumped.

When police arrest a suspect, his own computer can often be a valuable source of evidence against him – even if he thinks he has erased all the files that could land him in trouble. Experts like Jim Bates can bypass the normal controls on a system and search the entire hard disk for those incriminating files.

In 1995, just such "recovered" computer evidence convicted a wife-murderer. Police suspected an aerospace engineer living in California of poisoning his wife with cyanide – but her body had already been cremated so no post-mortem was possible. There was no normal forensic evidence so detectives called in computer experts from the firm of New Technologies.

The suspect had wiped his home computer of all files that might be of use to the police – or so he thought. He had reckoned without the computer skills of specialists Joe Enden and Michael Anderson who soon found a deleted text file containing the suspect's personal diary.

The diary recorded the husband's worries about his wife being unfaithful to him. His suspicions were his motive for murder and the diary helped obtain a conviction when the case came to court.

THE FIRST INTERNET ARREST

The Internet is a fascinating and ever-growing source of information that can also help combat crime.

The world's first Internet arrest took place in July 1997, when a Colorado traffic patrol stopped a car for speeding. Driving the car was an Australian man whom British police wanted to question regarding a murder in London. Hopeful Scotland Yard detectives had posted the man's description and details onto the Interpol web site only two hours before.

While routinely questioning the man about his car, the American patrol radioed the man's details into their local police station, whose own computer spotted that he was wanted for questioning.

Thanks to the Internet, British police had caught a murder suspect half-way around the world. This was the world's first Internet arrest but certainly not the last.

Many police forces and other law enforcement organizations now have their own websites on the Internet. The FBI have their own site (http://www.fbi.gov) that includes a section showing America's most wanted fugitives as well as pages on FBI case files, the FBI Academy, and major investigations under way at the current time.

The FBI clearly recognize the potential of the world-wide web and it can only be a matter of time before one of the killers on their "Most Wanted" list is caught thanks to the net.

The rise of computers and the Internet have created a whole new battleground in the fight against crime. As quickly as criminals find fresh and ingenious ways to exploit the new technology, detectives across the world will be finding ways to stop them.

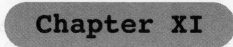

Chapter XI

The future of crime detection

Thanks to advancing technology and new scientific research, crime detection can only get better.

The biggest single breakthrough in the last hundred years has been the discovery and development of DNA-profiling. The idea that a suspect could be positively identified from only a tiny spot of blood or saliva or sweat found at the crime scene would have seemed science fiction only twenty years ago.

The possibility of DNA-sketching offers a revolutionary approach to the use of trace evidence. The technology may be twenty or thirty years away but when it arrives forensic scientists will be able to generate an impression of a suspect from his or her DNA that is almost as good as a photograph.

A SMARTER GUN

Computers and the Internet are certain to become an even more important part of everyday detective work.

Advances in microchip technology will allow the manufacture of Smart Guns – weapons which have a tiny computer inside them. The computer will analyze the fingerprints of the person holding the gun, and will only allow it to be fired if held by the registered owner.

In a fight or struggle, a police smart gun would be useless to anyone except the officer it was assigned to.

CAPTURED BY COMPUTER

At the moment, computers have great problems in telling one face from another. The complex features of the human face and the hundreds of different expressions that can pass across it make it an almost impossible task. Matching a face with photographs of a wanted criminal is beyond the capability of nearly all today's machines – but not tomorrow's.

Technology being developed at the moment should mean that in a decade or less, Computer Face Recognition (CFR) will be a reality.

In practice, this means that surveillance cameras in a city center shopping area, or at an airport or railway station, could be linked to a computer system. The cameras would scan the passing crowds, analyzing each face and comparing each one with a file of images of wanted criminals. If the computer spots a fugitive then an alarm signal would be sent to the nearest police patrol.

When CFR does eventually become commonplace, criminals will find it almost impossible to avoid capture.

VIRTUAL CRIME SCENES

A crime investigation is only as good as the evidence it gathers.

However thorough the team of forensic scientists are, valuable trace evidence can still be missed or ignored at the scene. After the scene is cleared for public access again, detectives get no second chance because the area will immediately be contaminated by new materials from outside.

To ensure that as much trace evidence as possible is gathered, future crime-scene officers could well be robots. They are not only more efficient than a human officer, but also faster at analyzing evidence.

Delays while evidence is being processed are a constant frustration to detectives, who know their best hope of catching a criminal or murderer is to act quickly. Any delay makes the detective's job even more difficult, as suspects have time to escape or cover their tracks.

Robot crime-scene officers would be able to record and analyze fingerprints, DNA samples, and other trace evidence at the scene of the crime.

Even before detectives leave the scene, prints and DNA will have been checked against the huge databases of known offenders held on computer.

A digital camera fitted to the robot would record the crime scene, allowing detectives to create it as a a virtual landscape on computer later. This simulated scene can then be explored and studied long after the evidence in the real world has been disturbed.

PREVENTION IS BETTER THAN CURE

Perhaps one day it will be possible to prevent some crimes from ever happening.

DNA gene-mapping may discover the gene that makes

one person turn to crime while another person in a similar situation does not.

Equally the work of psychological profilers already provides detectives with a guide to the background and history of people likely to become serial killers. Perhaps one day this tiny percentage of people can be spotted and guided away from that crime.

Psychic detectives could concentrate their efforts not just on solving crime, but on helping police predict where and when incidents will occur. If talented individuals can use their powers to locate bodies and find missing people, why shouldn't they be able to predict these incidents before they happen?

British psychic Nella Jones predicted the last attack of the Yorkshire Ripper months before he struck. The ultimate dead giveaway would be for police to know about a crime before it had even been committed.

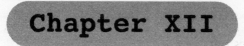

Chapter XII

The detective questionnaire

To be an effective detective you need a good memory, excellent powers of observation, and an eye for detail.

The following twenty crime questions are designed to test how good a detective or FBI agent you would be. All the information you need to obtain a perfect score is contained in this book.

Detectives have to respond quickly and under pressure during a investigation so you should allow yourself no more than twelve minutes to complete the test. All the questions are multiple-choice; simply write down the letter of the answer you think is correct for each question.

When finished, check your responses against the correct answers at the end of the questionnaire and discover what kind of crime investigator you would make.

QUESTIONS

1. "Lottery Kidnappers" Stephen and Megda Bradley were caught by Australian police thanks to the evidence of
a) a member of their own family;
b) a friend of the victim;
c) two types of cypress tree;
d) two off-duty policemen.

2. Psychic Chris Robertson receives his information while
a) at the scene of a crime;
b) in a trance;
c) asleep every night;
d) holding an object in his hands.

3. Identical twins have
a) identical DNA and fingerprints;
b) identical DNA, but different fingerprints;
c) different DNA but identical fingerprints;
d) different DNA and different fingerprints.

4. The first ever psychological profile was created by Dr. Brussel of New York to catch
a) the Railway Killer;
b) the Mad Hatter;
c) the Mad Bomber;
d) the Son of Sam.

5. Christopher Pile, the brains behind a complex computer virus, was known as
a) the Black Baron;
b) the Black Phantom;
c) the Blackmailer;
d) the Black Guardian.

6. In 1987, the British Home office set up a computer system called
a) Holmes;
b) National Crime Information Centre;.
c) Big Floyd;
d) Watson.

7. The world's first Internet arrest took place in July 1997 and involved
a) police in Spain arresting a man wanted in France;
b) police in London arresting a man wanted in New York;
c) police in America arresting a man wanted in London;
d) police in Australia arresting a man wanted in America;
e) a citizen in America spotting a man from the FBI website "Most Wanted" pages.

8. After Etta Louise Smith experienced a psychic vision for the first time she
a) was asked to help the police search for the body;
b) attempted to catch the killer herself;
c) led police to the exact spot using a mobile phone link-up;
d) was arrested and charged with murder.

9. The first-ever murder conviction thanks to fingerprint evidence was obtained in
a) Deptford, London;
b) Buenos Aires;
c) Australia;
d) Scotland Yard.

10. Bite marks played an important role in the conviction of which serial killer?
a) Peter Sutcliffe;
b) Ted Bundy;
c) Jack the Ripper;
d) The Son of Sam.

11. The Gun Alley Murder in 1921 in Australia was solved by which kind of trace evidence?
a) DNA;
b) Fibers;
c) Fingerprints;
d) Bite marks;
e) Hair.

12. The FBI's Behavioral Science Unit that profiles serial killers is based at
a) the FBI HQ in Washington;
b) a lab in Maryland;
c) Liverpool University;
d) the FBI Academy in Quantico.

13. The Kate and Margaret Fox spirit-rapping case of 1848 involved which of the following?
a) four murders on a country farm;
b) a missing witness;
c) a hidden gun, located by psychic means;
d) all of the above;
e) none of the above.

14. Would-be bank robber John Roberts was caught by
a) police who followed his dog home and arrested him;
b) a sock with an incriminating mudprint on it;
c) having his fingerprints removed;
d) asking a radio psychic for help;
e) having his name embroidered on the back of his jacket.

15. The first murderer ever caught by a DNA profile was
a) Alec Jeffreys;
b) Douglas Beamish;
c) Arthur Major;
d) Colin Pitchfork;
e) Lennie Wescott.

16. Psychic Nella Jones's first case involved which of the following? (Choose more than one)
a) locating a body;
b) a stolen painting;
c) lost skiers;

d) a cemetery;
e) all of the above;
f) none of the above.

17. Fingerprint evidence helped convict Steven Benson from Florida of which crime?
a) Kidnaping;
b) Car theft;
c) Murder;
d) Computer theft;
e) Multiple murder.

18. Stephen O'Brien from Maryland is a
a) computer crime expert;
b) FBI Special Agent;
c) psychological profiler;
d) animal DNA expert;
e) convicted serial killer.

19. The principle that "every contact leaves a trace" was coined by
a) Edmond Locard;
b) Edward Locadd;
c) Edmund Halley;
d) Edward Locord.

20. The first British serial killer ever caught by psychological profiling was
a) the Yorkshire Ripper;
b) the Ribbon Man;
c) the Blackheath Poisoner;
d) the Railway Killer.

ANSWERS

Score 3 points for each correct answer.
1. c   2. c   3. b   4. c   5. a
6. a   7. c   8. d   9. b   10. b
11. e   12. d   13. e   14. e   15. d
16. b and d – score 3 points each
17. e   18. a   19. a   20. d.

SCORES

40 and above – Top cop! You have an excellent memory and acute powers of observation. Phone the FBI and ask for an enrolment form now.

20 to 40 – A fair rating, but you need to pay closer attention to details to be a top crime-buster.

9 to 20 – You'll have to do better than this if you ever want to crack more than just petty crime. Have another look at the important chapters.

9 and below – You wouldn't recognize a dead giveaway if it stood up and slapped you across the face. Go back to chapter one and start all over again. This time with your eyes open.

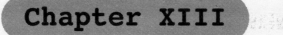

Chapter XIII

Chronological case list

Case: The Divining Rod Detective – Jacques Aymar
Date: Summer, 1692
Solution: By psychic's divining rod
Page: 39

Case: Body-Snatching
Killer: Burke and Hare
Date: 1812
Solution: Caught with victim's body
Page: 73

Case: The Fox Sister's Body in the basement
Date: 1848 – New York
Solution: By spirit-rapping
Page: 41

Case: Jack the Ripper
Date: Fall 1888
Solution: None
Page: 36

Case: World's first fingerprint murder conviction
Killer: Francesca Rojas
Date: 1892 – Buenos Aires
Solution: By thumbprint
Page: 17

Case: The Helpful Ghost
Killer: Alexander Drysdale
Date: September 1895
Solution: Assistant disguised as ghost
Page: 83

Case: First British Fingerprint Murder Conviction
Killer: Alfred and Albert Stratton
Date: March 27, 1905
Solution: Robbery & murder solved by fingerprints
Page: 18

Case: Button and Badge Murder
Killer: David Greenwood
Date: February 10, 1918 – Eltham Common, London
Solution: By badge and button left at scene
Page: 23

Case: Gun Alley Murder
Killer: Colin Ross
Date: December 31, 1921 – Melbourne, Australia
Solution: By hair evidence
Page: 25

Case: Bournemouth Murder.
Killer: Thomas Allaway.
Date: December 22, 1922.
Solution: By tire tracks left by killer's car.
Page: 21

Case: The Disappearance of Agatha Christie.
Date: December 1926
Solution: Psychic prediction
Page: 42

Case: The Murders at the Booher Family Farm
Killer: Vernon Booher
Date: July 1928 – Edmonton, Canada
Solution: By psychic means
Page: 43

Case: The Man with No Fingerprints
Date: 1930s – Texas
Solution: By lack of fingerprints
Page: 54

Case: The Poisoner's Gambit
Killer: Ethel Major.
Date: May 24, 1934
Solution: Post-mortem examination found strychnine
Page: 78

Case: The Case of the Countless Clues
Killer: Arthur Perry
Date: July 1937 – New York.
Solution: By excellent forensic work
Page: 52

Case: Luton Sack Murder
Killer: Horace Manton
Date: November 19, 1943
Solution: Good detective work, and fingerprints
Page: 12

Case: The Acid Bath Murders
Killer: John Haigh
Date: 1949
Solution: By dental identification of victim's false teeth
Page: 81

Case: The Mad Bomber
Bomber: George Metesky
Date: 1957
Solution: Bomber gave himself away in letter
Page: 29

Case: Lottery Kidnaping and Murder
Killer: Stephen and Megda Bradley
Date: July 7, 1960 – Australia
Solution: By rare plant spores from tree
Page: 26

Case: The Stolen Kenwood House painting
Date: 1970
Solution: Partly by Nella Jones's psychic skills
Page: 46

Case: The Campsite Murders
Killer: David Meirhofer
Date: 1974 – Montana USA
Solution: By psychological profiling
Page: 33

Case: The Teresita Basa Murder
Killer: Allan Showery
Date: February 21, 1977
Solution: By the victim speaking from the grave
Page: 85

Case: Radio psychic catches teenage killer
Killer: Owen Etheridge
Date: April 7, 1978 – California
Solution: By psychic means
Page: 55

Case: The woman who knew too much
Date: December 1980
Solution: Body located by psychic means
Page: 89

Case: Benson Family Car Bomb
Killer: Steven Benson
Date: July 9, 1985
Solution: By fingerprint evidence inside the bomb casing
Page: 20

Case: The Railway Killer
Serial Killer: John Duffy
Date: 1986 – London
Solution: By psychological profiling
Page: 34